A Certain Kind of Light

A Certain Kind of Light

by
Thomas Moore

QUEER MOJO
A Rebel Satori Imprint
Bar Harbor, Maine

Published in the United States of America by
REBEL SATORI PRESS
P.O. Box 363
Hulls Cove, ME 04644
www.rebelsatori.com

Book design by Sven Davisson
Cover design by Michael Salerno

Library of Congress Cataloging-in-Publication Data

Moore, Thomas, 1983-
  A certain kind of light / Thomas Moore.
     pages cm
  ISBN 978-1-60864-083-6 (pbk.)
  1. Teenage boys--Fiction. 2. Self-realization--Fiction. 3. Life change events--Fiction. 4. Psychological fiction. I. Title.
  PR6113.O648C47 2013
  823'.92--dc23
                                        2013026012

This book is dedicated to David Rylance, whose generous help during the editing process went above and beyond and to whom I will be forever grateful. I doubt that this novel would be here without him. The warmest of thanks are also owed to Rebecca Dyer and Michael Salerno, for their help and enthusiasm in reading the first drafts of the book and for their constant support and encouragement during this time. In memory of my parents, who will never get to read this.

1

"Are you ok?" I didn't mean that. Most of the time I don't wait for an answer. I use it as a greeting. It's more like a reflex. So basically I just said hello.

"Yeah."

Luke's dad died a week ago. Since then it feels like he's changed. His face looks different. I don't mean that in a deep way; his eyes aren't sadder; his expression doesn't look like he's had to deal with a lot of heavy stuff or anything, even though he has. I mean a real physical change. It looks like he's swapped faces with this kid that we know called Alex. I don't know for certain because Alex takes a lot of drugs and I haven't seen him for a long time. If I were to see him now though, I'd be expecting to see Luke's face. That's the only way that things could make sense.

No-one else has mentioned Luke's face, and this is the first time I've thought about it, actually. So I'm keeping quiet, because it could just be bullshit on my part, or because I'm really fucking stoned.

Luke's not really saying much, which is good, because I wouldn't know what to say back to him, apart from really obvious stuff like telling him that everything will turn out ok. He'll have heard that a million times by now. I'm tempted to say it anyway, out of nowhere, because coming from me it might make him laugh.

I'm looking away from Luke, and at the cup on the floor. I'm trying to work out why someone stuffed the bird inside it. It must have already been dead when that happened. It's all red and torn and pink between the feathers. I can only see little bits.

"It's too cold." Luke's neck has disappeared because his shoulders have hunched up.

"Where do you wanna go?"

"I want to sleep."

"Wanna get stoned?"

"No. Well, yeah, but I wanna sleep more. Or I have to sleep more than I have to get stoned."

The wind just spat real fast. The feathers shivered like someone just walked on the bird's grave.

Luke's hard to read. Even more so now. I hate the part of me that thinks I might be able to have sex with him because his dad is dead. It's more to do with how much I love him than how selfish I am; I'm almost positive of that. We've slept together four times, but we don't talk about it. I guess that means we understand life. It's hard to tell.

I used to feel bad about thinking about Luke when I masturbated. I could never work out why, because I knew that I found him attractive and I never felt bad when I tossed off thinking about other boys that I liked. I imagine I'm his girlfriend – this girl called Emma who I might be in love with too. Some of the things I think about are probably degrading, but I mean them with such veneration sometimes that it's just unbelievable, even to me. I scare myself with the amount of love that I have for the world. That's what I tell myself anyway. I tell myself that I'm lucky as if I'm talking to someone else. I think that's because I wish I was.

"It's the funeral in three days."

"Shit."

"I know." Luke's rubbing his hands together, but by the time that registers they'd disappeared up the sleeves of this really cool red and black check jacket that he's always wearing.

"Shall I come?" I feel stupid for saying that.

"I don't know. Yeah. It doesn't matter."

"I'll come." That feels stupider.

"OK."

"I'll call you tomorrow."

I can't stop looking at the bird. I want to turn it over. There are probably flies eating the flesh that I can't see. The sound of Luke's dwindling skateboard gives me goose bumps.

Emma is wonderful because she sees me as a really good person. I get the feeling that she sees me as sincere and vulnerable. I'm shy, but the other thing is I can still recognize what people think are my strengths.

I'm thinking about calling Emma because it's late and she'll be up and I feel pretty bad about myself. It takes awhile but I finally do.

"Hello?"

"Hey Emma."

"Oh hi." I can't make out whether she's been sleeping or if she's just tired. "How are you?"

"I saw Luke tonight."

"Yeah, he said." If Luke was there then she would have said so at that point. So they must have spoken on the phone. "It's been so cold today."

"I don't know whether I should go to the funeral."

"Did Luke ask you?"

"Yeah." Even though he didn't actually ask, I know that's what he probably meant.

"Then go." I can tell that I'm not going to get the sorts of things that I'd like to get from the conversation. It sounds like Emma might want to start talking about stuff that I don't feel I could intelligently listen to at the moment. So I tell her "ok" and hang up.

I never know what to do with myself at night. Two guys on television are arguing about death. I don't know but it sounds like they're both arguing the same point. One of the men is a writer. I've seen him before. I suppose he gets more money from TV appearances than from his books. Maybe that's why he always looks so pissed off.

The lights are off. Every time the camera cuts to a different shot the amount of the wall next to the TV that's illuminated changes. On the same wall as the light, I've got a collage made up of photographs of me and my friends at some of the different gigs and parties we've been to. The television keeps turning it sky blue. My favourite picture is one of me and Luke. We're sitting outside a tent at a festival. Luke's sunburnt and high and I'm grinning because I felt good that day. We're precariously close to each other.

A band I used to love are playing a song that meant everything to me about a year ago because I thought it was all about being inadequate and people not being able to see through ugliness. When I read an interview with the singer who said that he wrote it about falling in love with the most amazing person that he had ever met, it sort of stopped meaning so much. It felt like he didn't understand his own song.

Bands let people down. I feel let down by them anyway. There have been times that I've tried my hardest to relate to this stuff so that I don't feel so remote. I try to believe in things as hard as I can so that eventually I might actually feel a better way about them. Instead all it makes me feel like is that belief is dumber and deeper than I can capably imagine. I look at the light as I switch channels.

It's too late to get a drink, because it'd mean going downstairs and risk seeing my dad watching porn. I know he watches it because

I've seen the videos that he hides in the same drawer that my mom keeps her sewing patterns. I was about ten when I first watched one of them. I was old enough to be left at home when I was sick and had the day off from school. I can't remember what I was looking for when I found it, maybe matches. I watched a woman screaming while a black guy kept telling her how tight her pussy felt. Her head kept bumping the headboard. I found a magazine in his briefcase before that, though, a different time. I was playing a game where I pretended to be a spy and ended up finding a glossy A5 pamphlet of women who looked like casual teachers dressed unconvincingly as school girls.

I know my dad's drunk because I keep hearing the glass chinking on the bottle of whisky. It scares me how pathetic he is when he's like that.

Switch back. The band has finished their song and is being interviewed by a guy dressed younger than he is. I wonder if Luke's watching the same programme as me, because I know that he still likes the band. I don't call him in case he's managed to get some sleep. Maybe music is different for him now that his dad's dead. I'm curious but I won't ask him.

I'm looking at peoples' profiles. You can enter your postcode and it'll show you all the people who live near to you. I recognize quite a few. There's a boy who I always see in town. His page says that he's ninety nine, but I think he's about eighty six years younger than that. I thought he was a girl at first. I've thought about what it might be like to fuck him a few times. I don't think he knows how powerful he is. By the time people understand beauty, their bodies are usually way too gone. I only know that because my body is powerless, which means I have a better understanding of people who aren't. His page says that he is willing to talk to anyone but just because people say a thing like that, it doesn't mean that it's true.

The boy is called Craig. It doesn't suit him. He's skinny and he's got longish straight brown hair that's brushed across his face and I'm staring at his pictures like they're the only light left in the room, which now that I've turned off the TV, is the truth.

I'm imagining what it would be like if he and Emma had sex. The only way I could picture if is if I was Emma and I was riding the kid. In my mind he looks so exhausted and godly I can't make out my own place in it.

I worry that it's sexist to think that I'd make better use of Emma's body than she does. Maybe it'd be worse if I didn't admit that. I reckon I'd make better use of Luke's, too.

Craig's friends are hidden. The only ones I can see are the ones who have left comments on his pictures. I'm cross referencing people now. So many teenagers seem to think that the word Tragedy represents them – a lot of people seem to use it in their screen name. They're trying to make a point. It's like they decided collectively to torture themselves so they could feel less alone with one another.

Maybe the bird just fell from the sky. Although something about that doesn't sit right. Maybe it landed on a road and got hit by a car. I think about what sort of sound that would make. Maybe it was caught by a fox.

It looks like Craig didn't know the person taking the photo of him on his profile, or looks like he didn't trust them. Someone saw the chance to be close to him and tried to use the camera as cement. His hood is pulled up and he's just looks – blank? There's only two photos. The second is really small, like it's a thumbnail that's meant to get bigger when you click on it but it doesn't. I like that it implies he isn't vain.

This girl is sixteen and from America but talks the way a fifty year old man from England would think that a sixteen year old girl from New York talks. I don't know if what I said is true. Still, she says that Craig is beautiful, so it's not all lies. All of the comments on her page are from people asking if they know her or if they've met her. None of her friends are sure they know her like she's really familiar but her existence is confusing. Not that her friends couldn't be liars too. Everyone lies. I lied to Luke when I told him that he was just being paranoid about me wanting to sleep with him or sleep with Emma. Now I can't even remember what I said.

I'm looking at a photo of Luke now, like it will help me solve something. I know that it won't because I've looked at it before and it's given me nothing unless you count in lonely. After all I've looked for in it, it's like I've stripped it of its meaning. Luke would tell me shut up if he could hear me thinking this stuff. He says I over think things which is like telling me I hit my head as a kid and now I can't walk straight, but he isn't wrong, I know I do.

A man in a white coat is holding a scalpel and telling a lady who is faking an interest that he could transform her life. On another channel, a bomb has gone off and an actor has died. People are running and there are some cars that look really fucked up like a kid's had a tantrum and smashed up his toys.

I can't even pronounce the name of the country where the bomb went off, which makes me feel bad, so I concentrate on its spelling and sound it out in my head. As for the actor, he's in America. Everyone's saying he committed suicide but no one knows yet.

I'm looking at the phone and thinking maybe I should phone Emma again and just start talking about sex so she'll have to talk about it too if she wants me to stay on the line.

Whenever I've seen Craig around in real life he's been walking on his own and looking stoned. He's always out of sight before he gets to where he's going. I've never been close enough to make proper eye contact with him or anything like that. I think the last time I saw him was from a bus window which meant I only had a few seconds to see him before I moved on.

My dad's pissing, and missing the bowl most of the time, from what I can hear. When he's drunk he looks really insane; not dangerous though, just mad. I get annoyed at how stupid it makes him looks: staggering round in his boxer shorts, hunched over, squinting because he's taken his glasses off, all red and hairy and perplexed looking. I hate being able to see how afraid he looks. My dad doesn't have any friends.

I wish the walls were thicker so that I couldn't hear my parents' voices. I can't tell what the words are but I can still hear the sound that they make. My mother is most likely telling my father that he should drink less and my father is either telling my mother that he will or that he hasn't had a drink. I know a lot about my parents. I know that they're probably not in love anymore. One of the signs is the unhelpful things they always say to each other. I think closeness is to blame for a lot of things.

My mother's ill. She used to have cancer but now it's something else. Something to do with her lungs, she doesn't know what yet. She coughs a lot, especially in the morning and at bedtime. In the morning she usually throws up. The coughing annoys my dad because it's so persistent and loud. Sometimes it sounds so loud and weird that I think he thinks it's fake.

My parents must have argued because I just heard my dad walk back downstairs, and then I heard the cupboard open, and now the glass and the bottle.

My dad sleepwalks. When I was younger it would scare the shit out of me. I'd wake up from a dream and see him standing unevenly in my doorway, like he was shaken by what he could see. Because I was only half out of a dream, I'd be disorientated and my initial instincts couldn't do enough to sum up the situation properly, so my interpretation would be half dream/half reality and I'd think that someone wanted to kill me. Whenever that happened I'd feel like I couldn't sleep and that I had to stay on my guard all night. Even exhaustion the next morning didn't make me doubt I'd done the right thing. Since my dad became a drunk, it's felt like that again. One of these nights I'm convinced that he's going to slip on the stairs and snap his neck. I wonder if he'll be heading for my room when it happens. I feel cruel for thinking maybe he'd be happier if he died.

"Have I woken you up?" I went against my first plan.
"No. I can't sleep." That makes two of us then.
"What are you doing?"
"Nothing. Just sitting here."
"Me too."
"What's wrong?" Luke's perceptive or I'm obvious.
"My dad's drunk again but I want to go downstairs."

10

"Just go."

"I can't. He's drunk."

"Then don't."

"Are you ok?" There I go again.

"No."

"Are you drunk?"

"No. A little. Not like your dad or anything." I think that was a laugh at the end of the line. If it was then it wasn't meant to be mean. And if it was meant to be then it mustn't be actually because I didn't feel anything.

"Did you see Emma?" I don't know why I asked that.

"No. She said you called."

"Oh yeah, ha."

"You stoned?"

"No." I'm not, really. "Maybe a little." I decided to add that to make him feel at ease.

"I think she's getting pissed off with me."

"Why?"

"Because of my dad. I've haven't fucked her since he died."

"Why not?"

"I don't know. A lot of reasons. I just haven't felt like it."

I get this idea that maybe subconsciously Luke is worried about his dad's ghost watching him and Emma have sex. Luke's dad definitely wanted to fuck Emma. He always used to stare at her legs when she wore a skirt. I almost feel the words creep out of my mouth muscles and then stop myself because I realise just how stupid it would be for me to seriously suggest it. Instead I say:

"Do you believe in ghosts?"

"No." I didn't really think about whether or not I should even ask that, because I was preoccupied picturing Luke's dad fucking Emma. I had this image of him bending her over his sofa while a cigarette burnt itself out in an ashtray.

"Neither do I." Given the circumstances, it would be insensitive to say otherwise.

11

"Yeah." I don't know what Luke means because he sounds exonerated but I agree anyway. His breathing sounds heavy, like it's highlighting the alcohol. Luke looks good when he's drunk. It's just drunk older people that I can't handle. When I was young I used to hate people see transform. I never grew out of it.

"So are you going to come to the funeral?"

"Yeah. Definitely. Is Emma going?" That was stupid.

"Yeah." I'm thinking about Alex fucking Emma, now. Alex has got his own face which makes me realise how stoned I was before. Emma looks like Emma. She's really beautiful but I've said that already.

I wonder what Luke thought about the bird, whether he even noticed it. I don't know if he saw it. There's a programme that just started that's all about sex changes. I flip over again. Everyone on television looks so sorrowful.

I wake up and walk downstairs. There's cat litter all over the carpet. The cat is really old so he stays inside at night now, in case he gets lost in the dark or something. Our back garden falls back on some woods. My dad must have kicked the litter tray by accident and not realised how much mess he'd made. Same with the ashtray. There are tissues in the bin and when I turn on the TV, it's on a soft porn channel. It's off air, because it's 7am so there's just a test card of a blonde woman, and a phone number. The woman's hand is on her hip and the phone number has been designed so that it's really easy to remember.

I check Craig's page. He hasn't logged in today. It's early. I don't friend request him because we don't know each other, which actually makes things easier, I think, but not everyone thinks that. I look at his pictures again. They've not changed.

For about two seconds I suddenly feel so desperately fucking alone but then the phone rings so I forget that and answer it. It's someone asking for my mother, but she had to leave early for work so I tell them that and they ask if there's a better time to call. I ask who's calling but I'm so tired that I space out and end up hanging up because I figure before they can answer that it's probably someone trying to sell something.

My dad is snoring loudly. He'll wake up soon and start wondering round the house looking lost and pretending that everything is fine.

I feel like the walls are closing in so I grab a coat and go outside. I walk out of our street and round the back, into the woods, because I have nothing else to do. I sometimes go there to think but spend most of the time trying to forget things. The only person I see is an old man walking his dog around. It looks exactly like a dog that I always used to see when I was really young, but it can't be because that dog was already old then. Maybe the old man always buys the same kind of dog when the one he has dies.

I walk till I'm in a clearing that I always end up walking to. It's really wide and there are lots of bumps in the ground. I'm standing looking around. Luke and I sometimes steal booze from his dad's drinks cabinet and bring it here. One time we started a fire and I spent the night worrying that we'd not put it out properly and that my house would end up burning down.

I think about what I'm supposed to do today. I'm meant to meet up with this guy who used to go to our school until his parents moved him to a private school. We're not close or anything but we kept in touch on account of the fact that he phones me every six months. We usually just walk round town not doing much. I might talk to him about Luke because he doesn't know him that well, so it wouldn't matter what I say. Not that I'd say anything bad necessarily because I really don't know how I feel. It'd just be nice to have that freedom.

I wonder if the bird is still in the same place.

I think my mother wants me to go with her to the hospital. I hate going there but I think she appreciates the company either because she's scared or it makes her condition feel more real to the rest of us. Sometimes I don't think that she thinks we believe that she's ill. My family are all paranoid because they don't have the energy or heart to deal with each other. I'm starting to believe it's the same thing.

I've turned off my headphones because I want to hear the wind and leaves. Stuff crunches when I walk. Sometimes my foot sticks. I should have worn better shoes. I hate buying clothes. I'm wondering whether there was a reason why I came here but I know if there was one then it's not the sort of thing that I'd be able to sum up to myself. I've been trying to act more on impulse lately, or at least I've been thinking about wanting to act more on impulse. I don't think I've done it yet.

I think that I find the idea of acting on impulse hard because I don't really trust my instincts.

I'm home and my dad can't find his glasses. They're new. He got them a couple of weeks ago and they cost three hundred pounds. When I got in stoned one night he asked me if I liked them and he seemed really happy because he liked the idea that he might be fashionable, like he discovered he could genuinely do something with himself. I think that buying them made him feel special and less alone. I told him that I liked them but when I looked at him wearing them, I saw a sad, drunken old man with bad vision which scared me more than anything. Now he can't even find them.

He's saying that he can't remember where he put them, which means he was drunk and he's lost them. I'm trying to stay patient.

"They're usually in my top pocket so they must have slid out when I bent over."

"Where did you bend over?"

"I don't know. Ha ha. I was that tired last night that I can't for the life of me remember."

Dad's taken all the cushions off the settee and is looking there. I'm looking in the bin in the kitchen. It stinks of ash.

"So how are you?" He's got a sarcastic face; probably because it was such an obvious thing to say.

"I'm ok." That too.

His name's Chris.

"I saw Paul the other day," I don't know who that is.

"Oh cool. How is he?"

"Same old Paul." I'm guessing whoever it is, is fine.

"Good."

"Have you seen anyone?" He means from school.

"Not since the holiday started."

"I never know what to say – I avoid them, ha."

"Yeah."

"What have you been doing with yourself?"

"My best friend's dad died." I'm trying to decide whether to tell him about the bird.

"Fuck. That's really bad." I nod.

I just glimpsed someone else's newspaper for half a second. There's a headline about the actor.

"So how's your friend taken it?"

"He won't let his girlfriend fuck him."

He's looking at me like I just said something really strange.

"What do you mean? Because he's sad?"

"Maybe. No. In case his dad's ghost ended up watching them." That's not helped.

On the road outside the fast food place where we're drinking milkshakes, two motorists are shouting at each other. I can't work out what they're arguing about till I realise they aren't positive either so I'm within the loop. Chris didn't doesn't see, or doesn't care. It seems wrong to change the subject, even though I'd like to.

Chris reminds me of an animal but I'm not sure which one. Just his face. I think he used to hate himself, or maybe still does. When we were twelve and bored I offered him a blowjob and pretended to know what I was doing. When I slipped his jeans down, the tops of legs were covered in cuts and slashes like someone had given a toddler a red crayon and a piece of paper to work with. He didn't get hard the whole time and kept saying that he was only doing it because it would make his father angry if he knew. I can't remember whether I believed him, because I knew that his father wouldn't find out so it wouldn't make a difference. It was just before he switched schools so I didn't see him for a year after that.

I decide not to talk to Chris about Luke and Emma because it seems more pointless than *not* talking to him about them. I don't even know whether I want reassurance about anything anymore. I worry sometimes that they might both hate me because they can tell the sorts of things that I think about. I sometimes think that Luke hates Emma. I can't be clear beyond doubt that I hate anyone.

This whole day feels irrelevant.

"It's the funeral in a couple of days."

"Are you going?"

"Yeah. Luke asked me."

"Luke's your friend, yeah?"

"Yeah."

Every day I see an old lady sitting in exactly the same place.

She's on the second floor of a set of flats. There are only two floors, so I guess it's actually the first floor. The other is the ground floor. She's at the top, anyway. I see her through her large window every time I walk round to the bus stop. No matter how early it is, she's always awake. She sits in her chair. I can't tell if she's doing anything. It doesn't look like it. There's usually a blanket – it might be red – covering up her legs. The sight of her makes me feel terrible. I can never tell if she's looking at me. A couple of times I've been convinced that she was but the way her eyes work, anyone would think that.

"Are you ready?" I think he means to leave. We've been here an hour.

"Yeah."

Something about Chris makes me think about the old woman. Maybe they look like the same animal.

"It's been good seeing you."

"You too."

"I hope your friend feels better – and, you know – I hope the funeral is ...,"

"Yeah. Thanks." Just before he turns away, I'm struck by the animal that has so far eluded me. He looks like a meerkat.

Later, I'm sitting down looking at a tree on a concrete island in the middle of a road. Some punks just walked by trying to look like they knew where they were going and what their lives meant. Whatever.

If Luke had seen the bird then he would have said something. Maybe he did see it but compared to everything that's been going on with his dad dying and waiting for the funeral and not fucking

Emma, the bird just didn't seem to stand out that much.

I hate seeing photographs of people I care about before I knew them. I can't decide whether it's because I missed out on something or − something more complicated than their relation to me. The first time I ever went to Emma's house I felt really sad because it was like someone had made up this big museum made up of all the days that she's been alive that I didn't get to spend with her. I know I sound stupid.

"Where are we going?"

"Nowhere."

"OK."

Luke's driving his dad's car. The first few times he showed up in it, it scared the shit out of me, because there's no way he could fool anyone into believing that he's old enough to be driving it. Apparently his dad used to let him drive around these big fields when they used to go on holiday. It seems crazy to me because my parents are so normal, and stuff like that would really freak them out. But we've never been near big fields.

The road is halfway through having something done to it, resurfaced, whatever. It makes the car rattle. It sounds like someone shaking a tin box full of coins − only in slow motion, real slow, so any sharp sounds are muffled dull. It sounds creepy because it's getting dark and I'm stoned, or being steered that way.

"Is Emma coming?"

"No. She's busy."

"What's she doing?" Luke doesn't answer which means that he didn't hear me or doesn't want to think about it.

I'd like to see Emma. If she was here I might feel different. Luke looks like hell. The road looks almost beautiful. Nice light to be driving in. I sometimes forget how easy it is to get to the countryside. We've been driving less than an hour and we're already there. Driving past what must be farmland because there are long wooden fences and the nature looks neat. I'm pretending that my eyes are a camera.

"Good day?"

"I had to talk to people about the funeral. My aunt's sorting it out, I guess."

"You want me to come?"

"Yeah. I asked you." I don't know why I keep checking. Maybe I don't want to go, and if I ask permission enough, he'll change his mind. I love Luke so much.

"Do you know Chris?"

"Who?" That doubles as a 'no'.

"He was at school before you came. I met up with him today."

"What's he like?" I suppose it dawned on me that I didn't actually know.

"He's ok."

I keep wondering where we'll stop. Maybe we won't. Maybe we'll just keep on going until we disappear. Part of me hopes that that's the case.

"He said that he's sorry about your dad dying and that he hopes you're ok and that he hopes the funeral goes alright." That just fell out of me. The words got a little jumbled. It wasn't planned. Luke must know that because he hasn't answered me. Some tree trunks are making silhouettes like dying dinosaurs; diplodoci burning to ash.

I'm thinking about what would happen if I sent Craig a message online. I want to leave a comment under one of his pictures saying that I know exactly why he looks so afraid, if he is afraid. He must be.

People notice each other. Luke would probably recognize Craig if he saw the photo. He must have seen him wandering around at someone point. If I described him now, though, he wouldn't have a clue, *though*. It would only complicate things so I keep the question to myself.

Luke's driving us home now. We stopped next to this big field for about twenty minutes and rolled a couple of cigarettes and listened to some bad radio interference. I guess it was just something he wanted to do: drive away for an hour. Maybe he thought there would be more room to think without all of the stuff to do with his dad – the physical things like their house and his aunt and the funeral and Emma. Maybe he was just bored.

Luke drops me off at the end of my street and says something about calling me tomorrow. I can't remember if the funeral is then or the next day. If it was tomorrow he would say so now. It'd be rude if I had to ask. I know it's important that I'm there.

The car is gone and I'm pissing in the middle of the street. I could have waited till I got inside, because I was desperate but not so badly I couldn't hold out the extra few minutes. So maybe this is lazy? It was instincts; mine. Like I said, I'm trying to trust them more. My instincts told me that I should piss in the street. It was just a feeling that I let myself follow. It's late so no one is going to see me. I wondered whether it might be something sexual, like exhibitionism, but I think I just really needed to piss was enough to warrant the action. I don't feel turned on, so that's clear. My dick is smaller because it's cold. The more piss that comes out the more relieved I feel: a direct correlation that I realise I've been thinking about for far too long already so I go inside.

The sound is low because of the time. A lady is trying to convince everyone to buy a new car. I never realised that Craig had a little blog section on his page. There's only one entry. It says 'Sorry'. I click on it but I'm taken to a blank page with red writing that tells me that only Craig's friends can read his blog. It says I can send a friend request if I like. I can't or don't want to do that so I click back and search for other stuff.

Some website has posted jokes about the dead actor. They all reference his body – either the drugs that were found in his system, or the fact that he'll soon start to decay.

I think more about what Craig might be apologizing for and then I search my room for a lighter. Everything is a mess. I usually keep it quite tidy, but there are clothes on the floor and pots of pens that have fallen over, school work from last term and CD cases too.

My brother's screaming. The first time it was just a noise. I couldn't make out words. The second is a little clearer. One of the words is *fuck*. Definitely *fuck*. I open my door a little and call as quietly as I can to ask what's wrong.

"Nothing!" That was a snap. Really sharp.

"Are you sure? I heard ... "

"*Nothing!* Now just *fuck off!!!*" His voice gets higher towards the end of a sentence when he's angry like he's stretching upwards for something. I'm annoyed because he's had a bad dream and is blaming me for it because I'm the only person awake and I offered to help him. He calls me a faggot and then goes silent. I don't slam the door because my parents are asleep, but I hold the handle really tight after I shut it, until my fingers hurt. My jaw is tight and I'm trying to find the right words to scream in my head but none of them are adequate – not *fuck*, not even *cunt*. When I put them together they still feel weak. Words that predictable don't help anybody.

I'm thinking about whether people who work in morgues ever get star struck. When they undressed the dead actor, did the doctors feel nervous? Maybe the fact that he's dead makes it weirder. Maybe it makes it more normal; easier to understand. Maybe they just had a look to see how big his cock was. Someone has Photoshopped a picture of him. They've added worms and changed the shade of his skin. He's a dull cerulean blue now.

My brother is lonely too. It's a lot more obvious than with the others; by which I mean he doesn't try to hide it or doesn't know how. He's a natural result of this family, I guess. It makes me wonder about whether loneliness is hereditary. I found a lighter. I'm thinking about dinosaurs.

A message board says that the actor died after he finished having sex with a model. Emma would look amazing if the actor was fucking her while he was still alive.

My hands look better when they're busy. My right hand is holding a joint. It's between my fingers. If I squint I can almost imagine a twig hanging from a branch, ready to break off. I try and blow some smoke rings. After a few attempts I give up and just let the smoke take whatever shape it wants – impressions of clouds, probably some animals in there too, whatever – like drawing a picture with your eyes closed and then deciding what all the scribbles are afterwards.

Being stoned doesn't make things seem better or worse. It's got something to do with confusion. Maybe it makes my body feel just as confused as my brain – brings them into a more apt alignment. My body isn't great but when it doesn't work right, it's because I can't do something. My brain feels more awkward, like it has what it needs, but refuses on principle. Fuck it. They're both broken. None of that is accurate. Being stoned just doesn't make me any more confused that I already am; it simply diverts it.

My computer is the centre of the room again since I turned the TV off. The only sound is from the radio.

Someone somewhere will be thinking about the bird. Maybe it only came back to them when they sobered up. One time I think I told Emma that I wanted to kill myself. I don't remember if I meant it. Things matter one minute and don't the next. I try to make that happen as much as possible because I don't like having to deal with the stuff that sticks around.

I read an email from a friend. She's sent it to everyone. It's a puzzle. I have to stare at it for ten seconds and I'll see something appear. I'm staring at a black and white chequered pattern that's made up of itty bitty bitmap.

The email tells me to wait. I can't tell if the pattern is moving or if my eyes are lying because they're tired. Words appear and tell me to wait another ten seconds so I stare harder to try and move the time along a little quicker. I wait for ten seconds. I consider the pattern a little more. Maybe the movement is related to a blind-spot. So whenever I focus on a certain spot of squares then they stay still and the ones around it – the ones I'm not giving my full attention to – look like they're moving. When I look at those, they stop, and the ones I've just stopped looking at pretend to move, blurring but staying in the same place. It's all a trick. My eyes hurt but I keep on staring. Something appears telling me that I'm gullible for staring at the screen for so long. The email is a joke. It doesn't feel funny, so I close the email and reopen it. I watch the squares again. I understand the joke but that didn't feel too funny so I stare harder this time in case I missed something vital to another joke. The clip is the same so I watch it again. Nothing happens except my eyes feel more sore and red in the dark from staring at the fuzzy black and white arrangement that keeps pretending to move but never does. The punch-line was definitely that I waited a long time for something to happen and then nothing did happen. I think about my sense of humour and wonder whether the other people that received it would have laughed or not. I can't imagine other people laughing at the fact that nothing happens. It's as if the email is designed to be the spectator to its own joke. Maybe the movement in the pattern has been laughter.

I click a button to reply so I can tell my friend that her joke was lame. I stare at the blank space where I should compose my message and then cancel it because I realise how lame it would make me sound. Luke's email address was written somewhere at the top so he would have got it too.

Before I realised that the pattern was making fun of me, it felt like a piece of art. The repetition made it feel familiar and cold and distant and strange. I feel tired and start clicking on random links. Maybe the pattern is still art because I've read about some artists who have a great sense of humour and I've read that it comes through in the art that they make. I understand jokes in art, because it's something that I don't know much about, so that would explain – *if the pattern in the email was art* – why I didn't get the joke.

Sometimes I wonder whether I need to be more sincere.

I think about the title of Craig's blog entry that I'm not allowed to see. Maybe him being sorry about something could be a joke too.

2

There's a certain type of light that just sends me crazy. I'm sitting in it in the back garden, on a bench, lit up by our security light that helps keep suburbia safe from everything but itself, which means less and less seeing as it's intent on spreading everywhere. I'm smoking a cigarette and wondering about whether people will ever hold funerals online. I have this weird image of someone being cremated so that their ash turns into bitmap.

3

My mother is angry because I didn't pass on a message. Apparently the person I spoke to on the phone was calling from a doctor; more specifically: hers. I wasn't at home much yesterday and forgot that I was supposed to go to the hospital with her. The appointment was cancelled anyway. We're going today. Someone rang yesterday to make the change. I hung up on them because I thought they were trying to sell me something. They called back and spoke to my mother later, so I'm still not sure why she's as angry as she is. The obvious answer is that she thinks she's dying but I'm having trouble taking it like that.

To set up a new profile I have to set up a new email address. I'm registered with the same site that Craig uses but I haven't used it for a year, which is about as long ago as the site was originally in vogue. My interest peaked after a couple of months and I forgot my password. I'm floating anonymously somewhere now, I guess forever. If the site goes bankrupt then my page will disappear. I chose a stupid name anyway – and I used a weird picture instead of a photograph of myself. But if I did the same again, then I'd be able to talk to Craig without worrying what would happen if I passed him in the street. That feels like too much to think about at the moment.

For the first two hours of the day I fight the urge to call Luke. I want to talk to him and tell him that everything is going to be ok, even though I don't think it is, but use that to make it convincing, because at the moment it feels like he's thinking a lot about his dad which makes our friendship feel almost non-existent and I want to remind him that I can help him out with things like this, I mean, life.

I get the feeling that Emma isn't helping him much either maybe because he won't let her and I sense this is my chance to feel close to them both again.

The only way I can imagine Luke's dad being cremated is if I make it look like something from television. The camera would be at the bottom of the coffin, so that the shot is from his feet looking up at the rest of his body. The camera would have to be slightly raised. I don't know much about dead bodies; less than I do about living ones, at any rate, which are things that I think about a lot more. I'm sure that when someone dies their body relaxes and everything drops. They shit everywhere. I guess piss would come out too. And all the other ... stuff. Whatever else comes out, I mean. I'm sure there's more. The body would be cleaned up before it's put in the coffin. It would be dressed. What do they do with the face? Put make up on, I guess – subtle stuff. I think about Luke's dad's corpse wearing lipstick and eyeliner and stop because it looks horrible and part of me wants to laugh at just how horrible it is which makes me feel guilty.

Dead bodies are all over the internet. Someone says they've got a picture of the dead actor, dead, so I look but it's nothing really; another joke – just an old photo of him with fake stitches and crosses drawn over the eyes. There are some dead actors on there, actually as corpses: one that I thought I was in love with when I was eight years old because he was in a film playing the sort of character that I thought I would like to be friends with at the time. I tried to shape all the other boys my age into someone like him at that point, with the way that I thought about them. He was probably about fifteen then. He had a certain expression on his face – like he was mad, only he wasn't good at being angry, so he looked more crestfallen than anything else; a mixture, I guess. Craig has the same kind of look about him. Maybe that's why he's sorry.

27

It's crazy how you can make people seem like exactly the person that you want them to be if you think about it enough. Sometimes I don't think I think about anything else.

Someone told me that ashes are a lie. Apparently when a family gets given the urn at the end of the funeral, it's only a little bit of the person that they think it is. I was told that they burn all the dead people together, and the ash all just gets split up, so you don't know who you're keeping the pieces of. If you're lucky then I guess you might end up with a couple of handfuls of what's left of the person you loved.

I don't call Luke because he probably has lots to sort out today, and if he hasn't then it probably still feels like he does.

"Will you be ready to go in an hour?"
"Um ... yeah."
"I don't want to go on my own. You know I hate hospitals."
"Yeah ... um ... I'll be ready. I just need to phone someone."
"Is it the funeral tomorrow?" I don't like it when people ask

questions they know the answer to. I do it sometimes, which is probably one of the reasons why it irritates me. Self-suggestion.

"Yeah."

"How's Luke?" I think about the question and all I know is that he's been driving around late at night doing nothing and not sleeping with his girlfriend.

"He's ok."

"Well, tell him I'll be thinking of him." I won't pass that on because it doesn't feel like it means anything. It's like this recorded message of sorrow, not awful or anything, but hardly worth repeating, seeing as you aren't likely to hear its opposite.

"OK mom," I say.

When I squint I can see rainbows through butterfly wings. A lot of the things I feel are things that I don't choose to feel. I just ... feel them, I guess. I don't want to feel more of the things that I feel. Sometimes I worry that I'm evil.

I don't call Luke and I try and avoid my mother until we have to go the hospital because seeing my parents makes me depressed, especially recently. It feels like something has to happen but nobody wants to work out what that is. My mother makes a couple of jokes at my father's expense, which I think means he was drunk last night.

All the stuff with the bird doesn't seem to bother me at the moment. Maybe because when I'm sleepy, other stuff becomes important. There's a slight overhang from a dream I had – a feeling more than a memory. I don't know what it was about. It was probably about forgetting things. In my dreams I'm always forgetting something or looking for an object, like a bag or a rucksack that I've left somewhere and need to go back and fetch. Sometimes I don't think dreams mean anything. Other times I think dreams are everything that can be. I like how people get swapped around in them, especially bodies. So I can be kissing one person but knowing that it is someone, maybe everyone else.

I keep highlighting chunks of text. Click and drag. Not important words. Mostly words I've not read. They're just there. Some people bite their nails, which is like what I'm doing.

Craig has logged in. It tells you that on his page. I think about what he might be doing and who he might be talking to. It strikes me how long it's been since I've seen him walking around. Because I hadn't seen him on the internet the last time I saw him in person, it didn't feel as important as it does now. I think that most of the times that I've seen him have been at weekends, on Saturdays mainly, like it's his personal day of rest.

If you don't add a photo of yourself then you just have a grey silhouette on your page, in the shape of a person's head and shoulders. I've made the page but I'm not thinking too much about it. I'll leave it for a couple of days and then decide whether or not I want to send Craig a message and also what sort of thing I'd write to him. His two pictures have a couple more comments, both from American girls. One wants to know something about computers, I think. It's hard to tell. The comment is cryptic and could also be concerning a secret. The other is saying really obvious things. They both look a little younger than Craig, maybe eleven or twelve. They live on different coasts and have different last names but they look eerily alike, as though they were separated sisters.

The noise that the match makes as I light it and the flame as it bursts into existence sounds like a miniature symphony. If the window is open and the cushions are pushed in at the bottom of my bedroom door then it won't bother anyone that I'm smoking because they won't be able to smell it.

Sometimes this stuff makes me feel sick and at other times it's fine. The first drag is nice and I'm looking at the clouds, which today are moving fast. It must be close to chaos up there. I wish I was in an aeroplane. The sky is grey so often round here that when the sky is blue it looks like the buildings have been superimposed onto them – like in a programme I saw about how special effects are made in films. When it chances to comes out, the Sun looks fake too.

So I'm smoking and listening to some strange scuttling sound. A bird has made a nest in the guttering of the house, which is right above my bedroom window. I picture a weird little baby bird with no feathers, all blind and pink, stretching its neck and opening its mouth, working each time on the premise that the stuff that appeared in it before and tasted good will abruptly be there again.

I can hear a basketball bouncing on tarmac. It sounds like a pair of huge elastic bands being twanged. The boy across the road is playing on his parents' drive. We have net curtains so I can't quite see his face through the sunlight and threads, but I can see the shape of him moving round and reflecting everything. I see him on the bus a lot. He's usually coming home from school. He flashes two second glares at me. He's older than me, maybe he's 18. He's usually with his girlfriend, who looks like a really dolled up social networking page that's passionately come to life.

Emma calls but I don't answer even though I'd like to speak to her. Sometimes I feel angry at her, but I'm not honest enough with myself to think about the reasons, only to notice they're there.

Downstairs my dad is asleep on the settee. I walk into the garage to put some empty tins in the recycle box that the local council gave to every household to encourage us to do our bit to stop the planet from dying as quickly as it is. Most of the bottles in there are whisky bottles. My dad has hidden a couple more under a work bench. It seems stupid to hide two of them, like knowing he'd got through 10 would be worse than knowing he'd got through 8. It suggests a totally skewered sense of shame. He was drunk when he hid them, so they're easy to spot. The carrier bag that they're in is unravelling slowly. Maybe he keeps them for an emergency although I have trouble trying to work out what the emergency would be. No doubt something emotional.

My dad would sleep there all day if nobody wakes him. It's almost like how a pet acts. My mother knows this and says something louder than she normally would which wakes him into a daze of pretending to agree and to comprehend the conversation.

I'm going to the hospital with my mom because my dad has to wait for something to be delivered. I don't ask what it is because I don't think that we need any more things in the house than we have already. Maybe the new things make them feel better sometimes. Or maybe each new item is a gamble. Maybe it isn't even about the odds anymore. Maybe someday it will all fall into place.

Craig looks so intense in his photos, but in this way that's probably more intense to look at than to actually feel. He looks so bored that it hurts, as if by just looking at him for the length of time that I have been I'm boring him even more. His body is important, whether he knows it or not, which I'm presuming he doesn't. The bird felt important. The funeral is important. Emma and Luke are so important that it makes me want to disappear.

The screen tells me that I've been logged out due to inactivity. I get distracted easily. I go other places. I leave things behind.

When my parents ask me questions I always feel like everything collapses inside me. I drink a large glass of water in one go and my eyes well up. The garden looks strange, probably because it's the only thing here that looks alive. They've tried to mute it, I think.

"How are you getting to the funeral?" That was my mother. She's playing a Gameboy and not looking at me when she talks.

"I'm walking. Or I can get the bus."

"I can drive you if you want." Her eyes dart around a little bit, following whatever character or cursor she's controlling. Her cheek twitches. Maybe she jumped off a ledge.

"No that's fine. I think I might like the walk." I could smoke something on the way if I can convince myself that it won't make me feel bad.

My mother doesn't answer, so I repeat what I said. "It's ok, Mum. I'll be fine walking." Alright, so I changed what I said then.

Her eyelids ascend like she's widening her eyes to take in something but her pupils stay fixed. Her head lifts a tiny bit, so small that I only notice because I happen to be watching her. That's her response. I stand for another second and watch as she frowns down at the rectangle in her hands. She puffs a sigh. Maybe she died.

There's something about mornings that seems to throw me. I have to relocate myself every time I wake up. Check myself. Remember everything my dreams have tried to change or make me forget.

I think about how I'm more familiar with Craig's photograph now than I am with him in real life. I've lost count of the number of times that I've looked at his pictures. The encounters between me and the flesh version of his body must still be in single figures; early ones, too. Okay, I guess I've lost count of them too.

Thinking about Emma is hard for me. She makes me feel obvious. I see things in her that I don't like in myself. I see her relationships with other people and it makes me see how I am with her. She makes me transparent, see-through to myself. I don't like seeing myself the way I do her. She makes it harder for me to lie to myself, or she makes it harder for me to lie to myself without thinking about the implications. But then I think about this whole other life she lives when I'm not around and the comparison I'm making starts to make no sense. It's plain she has nothing to do with me.

I'm back in my room. The boy with the basketball just kicked it against the wall because he couldn't do a trick. That's a guess. I only looked just as the ball pinged back off the red bricks from really close to him, almost grazing his head. He let it bounce behind him, its springs up and down getting gradually smaller, closing the gap, hopping. The basketball sounds like a tribal drum and the boy looks like a warrior. His face is red and his blonde hair looks sweaty. He just cursed. He looks taller than before. People age and others hardly notice.

I'm sticking with the silhouette for now. I can find a picture to use later on. I'm just setting up the basics. I notice a picture of a girl lying on a bed. She's wearing a pink bra. Her hand must be holding a camera. Her face is trying to do something, look appealing or whatever it can manage. She's probably fifteen. The room behind her is a mess – probably the clothes she took off to look sexy. Underneath a handful of men have written that they want to fuck her, that she's pretty, that they'd like to fuck her and she's pretty. The next picture is her baby sleeping in a pram wearing a woolly hat that could cover its whole face if you wanted to pull it down that far.

When people aren't with me, I wish that they didn't exist. This frightens me, so I make things up. I've only been to Emma's house a few times. It never seems like a viable option. Last time she was lying on a bed tapping away on her laptop. She was looking at pictures of a dress. Her dad doesn't make me feel welcome. Because he wants to fuck his daughter and because she probably wants to fuck him, he assumes that any male who is in his house wants to fuck his daughter as well. I want to fuck his daughter. It's one of the things that I understand. I don't know why I'm convinced that he wants to fuck her, but I am. Part of me wants him to fuck his daughter just to prove me right but I'll ignore that until I understand things better or I die.

Emma is one of the people I find hardest to work out. Maybe when I think I understand other people it's always a lie. With Emma I can't seem to trick myself. The more she reminds me of myself the harder it is for me to think about her.

It doesn't bother me much when I think about her with Luke. Sometimes it's a turn-on but other times it's nothing. When I think of her with other people, though, it fucks me up. I get the feeling that Emma knows the sorts of things that I think about. Sometimes I wish that she didn't. I wish I could retrace the footsteps of our friendship so I could change certain things early on so that some people would look at me in a different light. People get the wrong idea. It's another way of saying they know me.

My father is watching television. There was just something on about the dead actor. My mother looks up from her Gameboy, over the top of her glasses and says that it's a shame that he's dead because he was young and had a promising career ahead of him. I don't think she's ever seen any of his films, but that's what all the people on the radio have been saying so I guess she got it from there.

When Luke's father is cremated, will he look scared? Are dead people still afraid? I mean, if they're anything. I can't imagine not being scared. That's why death's so scary.

"Hi Luke,"

"Hi."

"What are you doing?"

"Not much. Drinking. What else? Ha-ha."

"Haha." We both know *that* it's not funny. Luke sounds ... something. Some words.

"What about you?"

"I'm stoned. What else?" He didn't laugh at that. Now I feel stupid. I move us on:

"I've gotta go to the hospital soon."

"With your mum?"

"Yeah."

"Is she ok?"

"I think she's worried about dying. I think she hates her life a little." Luke doesn't really answer that. There's some noise nearby him, but it's ... nothing? It sounds like he could be smoking.

Without anything else to say, I reach for what's there. "Oh listen, she told me to tell you ..."

"Yeah." Luke interrupts me. His tone is predictable. "Tell her thanks." He must have had to say that so many times, like he's been getting gifts.

"When do you have to go?" That's him.

"Soon. Do you have, erm, stuff to organize today?"

"Not really. Good job, too, haha"

"Haha."

"My aunt has done everything. I think Emma wants to come round. She's called five times but I haven't answered."

"Why?" I don't want to know in a way.

"I don't know. What's that noise?"

"Oh – it's a boy that lives across the road – he's playing with a basketball. He's kinda hot, actually, ha. Well he's not, but he is when he's playing basketball, if that makes sense."

Luke doesn't answer. Maybe he heard a different sound. Sometimes he ignores me when he doesn't want to listen. It's like he's equipped with a switch.

Luke never had a page. He uses his computer a lot but he never seemed interested. Probably because he got to have sex with Emma, so that stuff didn't matter as much.

While I talk to Luke I open up the internet. I look at the email and at the squares that are pretending to move. It's so obviously an illusion now I become embarrassed.

I ask a couple of things about tomorrow and Luke answers me and we both know that our conversation has veered into the transparently meaningless. Sometimes I'm too scared to let go of people. Luke is more direct. He seems more so now than ever. It must be because of his dad. He knows that people die now definitely and that must fuck things up. I know that people die but both my parents are still alive so, of course, I don't. My brother is alive. Luke is alive and Emma is alive. Luke's father is dead.

"What?"

"Erm ... I don't remember." I think I said something.

"What do you mean?"

I can't answer that because I can't think what I said.

"What the fuck, man?"

"Erm ..."

"Are you totally stoned or something?"

"Pretty much. I guess I am, yeah." I feel like I don't know anything about myself or anyone else.

Luke says he'll call me later and hangs up. There's a slight slam of plastic before the dial tone cuts through. I might have annoyed him or maybe whatever I said was okay and his dad dying might have fucked him up. Fucked him up more than before, I mean. I don't know. This is all so ... nothing.

My dad takes tablets after every meal. I don't know what they're for. I'm saying this because we just ate. They're in a cardboard packet. Lots of them all in a silver wrapping shoved in with a piece of paper – folded up directions, ingredients. I read the packet but the words aren't worded for me – all medical terms and numbers – so I don't take them in. The pills are really big. He swallows one with a gulp of apple flavoured squash. There are microscopic tidal waves inside the glass because his hands are trembling so much. I can't believe I can see them.

My mother tells me to get ready so I put on a coat. My father says that he would have driven her to the hospital if he didn't have to wait for the washing machine to arrive. That's what's being delivered. He says that it's a pain because when something is being delivered, the people delivering it don't give an exact time for their arrival; they just say expect us between these set hours, like that period is dead air on TV waiting for a test pattern. I don't think he's really justified in being angry about it, though, because I doubt he would have gone out anyway. People look for things to blame.

Our new neighbours are on their drive loading cardboard boxes out from the boot of a silver car that looks a lot like ours and into their porch. The lady who used to live next door died of a brain tumour. She was my mother's friend and my mother cried at the funeral, but I wasn't there because I had an exam that day so I didn't see it myself. One of my other neighbours – the lady on the other side of our place – told me about my mum crying. She whispered it in my ear, like it was something I wasn't supposed to tell anyone but was meant myself to hear.

The house has been empty now for just under a year. There were legal things that had to be sorted first. I know that because I heard my mother telling somebody about it over the telephone six months ago. She pays attention to stuff like that and I guess so, apparently, do I. The new family smile and say hello and my mother replies. Her eyes quickly skim over them. Mine don't because I'm stoned and don't want anyone to look at me too closely but I'm pretty sure that there are two adults and one teenager, and two other kids, although one of the kids might be another teenager too. Once we're off the drive I don't look back. I figure I'll find out another time if it matters. There's a limit to my attention, in that case, or a lack of urgency.

The weather is fucked at the moment. One day it's sunny and then the next it looks like it might snow. It's because the planet is dying. Some of the celebrities on TV have been saying that we're all to blame but I find it hard to take them seriously. I gaze out the window. All the houses here look the same.

I wonder where Luke's dead father is at the moment. I mean, who keeps the body till it's ready for everyone to say goodbye to it. It was a heart attack that did it, nothing irregular. Dead is dead however I think about it. The only deaths that feel different are murders or something fucked up. I don't know anyone who's died like that, so I'm only guessing. Strange how heart attacks don't seem fucked up. Maybe they do to Luke.

Before long, we're getting into town. It never takes that long to get to somewhere that you don't want to go.

We've stopped. Traffic lights are red. There's an old man walking across the road really slowly with a carrier bag filled with canned food, and it makes me feel stupid, like I want to cry. Little things throw me.

I'm looking at an old garage. It used to sell motorbikes but it's closed down now. I think there was a fire. I can't see very far inside because the sun is so bright in my eyes. All I can see in the window is a reflection of my mother's car. The walls have been fly-postered with orange sheets with details of an upcoming gig on them. I might ask Luke and Emma if they want to go. I don't enjoy seeing bands anymore because I can't concentrate properly while they're playing. After the third song I'm usually wondering how much longer they're going to be. Luke probably likes the band.

I notice a building that I've never seen before. Or a wall I hadn't seen. In front of it is rubble. Another building has been pulled down in front of it. That's why I couldn't see it before. It's the side of the old hospital. It's a listed building, which means nobody is allowed to pull it down, maybe forever. I can't remember what used to be next to it. I can see the dust and mess that it was made from. It's like a kid has messed up a jigsaw and left all the pieces in a pile. It's so easy to not pay attention to everything that's around you.

We pull up at the hospital. As soon as we go in, all of the bleeps that I can hear mean that people are being kept alive. The place sounds like a computer game. It's little bit like an art gallery too: all white and full of people frowning.

My mother says something to a lady sitting behind a glass divider. The lady stares down at something that I can't see and writes something really quick that I also can't see. I think that's her answer.

We migrate to the waiting area. A girl a little older than me just got called by someone out of view. I didn't hear her name, just the summons. My mother picks up a magazine and pretends to read it. She holds it in front of her then brings it closer, then puts it at the same distance from her eyes that she started at. The cover says that the magazine contains one hundred per cent true stories, which I think sounds strange, but I lose track of why because I start thinking about something else.

The side of the bird that I didn't see must have totally rotted by now. I imagine worms snaking in and out of the bird's body and think about the fact that it's usually the other way around, the birds that eat the worms. Then I think that actually maybe worms eat birds all the time – dead birds, anyway – and maybe people just don't see it. Every single bird dies. Every worm dies. But not every worm is eaten by birds. It almost adds up to something. I realise I'm still stoned.

This place is too clean. I think that I see a girl who used to go to my school. I'm not sure because she looks a lot like a few people I know, or I conflate those few people together. She looks like she'd be polite to me if I spoke to her but in a really blank way, like it wasn't about being polite but confused.

There's a drinks machine at the start of a corridor. I walk over and put my hand in my coat pocket, hunting for money. My fingers feel dusty. Old bus ticket stubs. Scraps of wrappers. I take out the coins I find. I sort through them. I put the ones back I don't need. The machine is so bright. I put two fifty pence coins and one twenty pence coin into the slot. They clatter somewhere. One comes back out. I put it back in. It clatters and comes back again. I try and push it in differently but my options are limited. Clatter. Comes back. Clatter. Comes back. My throat is tight. Too hot. I just hit something. The machine? Its brightness isn't helping me see. I put my hand back in my pocket and try another coin which works and suddenly I feel better.

To get a drink you have to look at its code and push that code in using the buttons at the side. I get a can of Coke. A couple of things click or whir or something, mechanical thinking, and the result is that the can bangs into the tray at the bottom. I wonder how many things have to go on inside the machine to make that happen but then stop trying to work it out because even if someone explained it to me, and even if it was only a few things, I wouldn't understand. A woman behind me looks annoyed that I've been standing in front of the machine for so long so I step away and snap the ring pull and swig. The coke makes my mouth feel gritty because it's not that long since I brushed my teeth. I put the can on my forehead to cool it down and wish that I hadn't because it ends up making my forehead wet. To fix that problem, I wipe my face on my sleeve.

The hospital is decorated with posters which serve as warnings. People are going to die if they don't do a list of things: Fat people and people who smoke and people who drink and people who take drugs. The list goes on. Luke's dad smoked and drank but he wasn't fat and I don't think he did drugs. I imagine Luke's dad stoned and turn my head because it looks too weird and so I need to look at something else.

I can't relax. It's because of the hospital. I don't know why my mother is here – having a test or getting results. She might have told

43

me earlier. I can't remember. In my mouth, there's the strong taste of sugar.

Someone must have to restock the machine every day. Someone else just got a can of coke. The same as mine. We've been waiting awhile.

When I think about Emma, I kid myself. If I were straight with myself then I'd know that there's nothing deep there – I don't mean in Emma, but in the way that I tend to think about her. The depth in her is a coastline that recedes whenever I approach it. The thing with me and Emma is an impression of something, or possibly a projection. Both ways. It's hard to tell what hurts when I think about her like this. Something in my chest. Further in than that. So far in that it's outside of my body. I don't know. I'm so bad at unpicking words.

When I finish at the hospital I might call Emma. I don't want to be at home so I might go to town. She could meet me. I imagine Emma being fucked by Craig, only this time he's more dominant, like he isn't strictly under my imagination's control. I feel like crying.

It's hard to tell who's dying in here. People look pretty much the same, unless something is especially bad; or someone's especially old. I think about the old lady who I see through the window, staring out from her flat. Some days I don't notice her, she's just so there. I wish I could never notice her. I might finally feel better if I didn't. I try not to feel bad about what that might mean for her. If she saw me the same way I see her, I might feel upset but it'd make no difference. I'd only want her to get away from having to see what she saw. I'd want her to wish the same thing for herself.

We're back in the car. My mother is talking about what the doctor said. She has to have more tests. She starts off a lot of sentences with "Well, like the doctor said…" like she's trying to win a debate. We're not arguing. I don't think we are. We can't be because I'm not talking. I'm listening. I'm half listening, but there are no real answers to anything she's saying so I don't need to listen properly.

The car stops at some lights. I want to get out and walk off somewhere but I can't because I know that would upset my mother and she's sick. I look at the sky instead. I have to squint. I'm tired. I want to put the radio on so we don't have to talk to each other, or I mean, so she doesn't have to talk to me.

"Are you ok if I put the radio on?"

She turns it on for me.

I'm thinking about avatars. I don't want anything that would be too obvious. I think a cartoon would be best. Maybe a gif. that moves a little bit on a constant rotation, with a pause to reload. There's a feeling that I want, but I can't put it into words. My mother says something about Luke and I think about his dad and I agree. There's no point not to. For a second I think she wants to come to the funeral and I panic more than I thought I would, which surprises me. I misheard her. She's not coming to the funeral. I wasn't properly listening.

People must think about funerals in different ways. Some people know more dead people than their friends do. That'd change things. I'm not too worried about being sad because I doubt if I will be but I am worried about things feeling too much. I don't know who is going to be there apart from Luke and Emma and Luke's aunt. I'd not thought about that until now, the guest list. I don't think I know anyone else who would go. Hopefully after the funeral Luke will want a break so we can go somewhere else and get stoned and pretend that his dad isn't dead and we can be stupid and Emma can hug Luke and me and I can pretend that we're all in love with each other, in the way that I've always wanted.

I feel lonely all of the time. Sometimes I forget but then I remember again. So that holiday doesn't count. I can't tell whether Emma and Luke are lonely. They have each other, but that doesn't prove anything. I get worried that they're making me feel lonelier by being lonely together. That doesn't make sense so it's probably true.

My dad seems drunk. It's hard to tell. Sometimes when he wakes up he's confused, either that he's woken up or about where he is. Actually, there could be a million reasons. He'd been asleep in front of the TV. He does that a lot now. More than before. He has more time now. I think he hates it. He hates it or he's scared of it. Maybe scared. I find it hard to imagine my dad hating stuff. I find it hard today anyway. I'm all over the place. If he hates anything then it's probably my mother. And most likely because she's scared.

My dad asks my mother how she got on at the hospital and she tells him some of the things that the doctor said. My father just agrees like he knew that stuff already. My mother says a few things that don't make sense. Or they do and I'm not listening properly again. I think it's that.

The basketball is still bouncing around outside; that kid's been playing for hours and his face looks flushed) and puffed. He's sweating. I wonder how many friends he has at school. He's not playing up for anybody at the moment because he doesn't know I can see him. He's doing what he wants to do for no one else but himself, or it's just the ball that matters, and something about that is amazing.

My mother just asked if the washing machine was delivered. My dad doesn't know. He might in a minute. At the moment everything he sees is probably still blurred by little bits of dream. That sounds nicer than it is. The boy just jumped up and a tiny bit of his t-shirt clung to his back and stayed there. Now his feet are back on the ground.

"So what are you going to do now?"

I don't know whether that was aimed at me or my father. Either way, I don't answer. I walk upstairs and rub my eyes. I feel half worn out. Maybe dreams are catching. That's not as nice as it sounds either.

There's so much crap on the bed. I push it onto the floor. I have to tread over CD cases and newspapers to move in any direction. I turn the computer on and look out the window while it loads up. Every few seconds I can only see the ball. There's a bush at the top of his family's drive that makes the kid disappear. He pops in and out. Gone. Back again.

The computer loads fast because it's new. Or it was, not so long ago, and it's still within the range of working well. I use it a lot. It doesn't make things better but it distracts me enough when I need it to. Although sometimes I don't think I'm in charge of when that is.

There's a little picture of a folder in the top corner of the screen. On the pretend inside of the folder there are lots of other pretend folders. I try and keep things in order. I don't know why, which means there must be a reason lurking in plain sight somewhere. I click on one of the folders and thumbnail pictures of pornography

47

appear. Some are videos. I don't have many. I click a few times without thinking too much. I'm already hard because the boy outside looks so flushed and puffed.

The sound is off. It makes it seem less real. It's not real. Most things aren't. I mean, statistically. The actors look like they've been hypnotized. Hypnotists must want to do stuff like that all the time. I'm on my knees. The people in the video aren't really hypnotised.

I already said that we have net curtains. We've always had. I think I heard someone say that they're not as common as they used to be. You don't see too many. I'm used to them. People not being able to look inside isn't about secrecy. It's about relief. Maybe people want people to see inside more nowadays because they think that it's safer. There's a difference between seeing inside and going inside that's coming apart.

The people on the computer are barely there. I'm not looking at them. Maybe they're not really fucking unless someone is watching. Like trees that fall in forest and the sound they're meant to make. The ones that nobody hears ... or ... something ... Maybe that's why I want to fuck people, mainly Emma and Luke; to prove I'm still here, in the senses of someone else. To make it a point I still matter.

I cum quickly into my hand and slump back at my desk. The porn hasn't stopped.

4

When I look at porn I have to try and turn down certain parts of my brain, or turn *up* other parts up. The actors are always older than I'd like them to be. But also, if I'm going to masturbate, I think I've figured out that I'd much rather look at photographs. Videos can be hot, if that's just what you're after, but photographs feel closer to the confusion or something that hangs on sex because I don't know what happened either side of the millisecond that I'm currently looking at. I'm not really even talking about photographs of pornography. I just want to look at people in their normal clothes, or with a slightly dumb look on their face, like they've just been caught out by whoever has the camera, or like they haven't noticed its existence at all. I don't even think that I prefer to see people doing sexual things, like I could just look at a kid standing with his skateboard or sitting on a bench looking worn out and staring at nothing, and that can totally bring me off in this way that feels more magical and closer to something I almost understand than any endorphins could possibly impress me. Or even if I don't get off, which is most of the time, at least it's closer to accepting all of the disorientation and substance that makes up being alive and feeling things, which is what always leads to sex anyway. I'm not sure what this means but the bottom line is this. Sometimes life only works if I think about it as a series of photographs.

5

The smell of my mother's perfume always used to make me think of places I didn't want to go. Now it makes me think of what it used to remind me of. They're different. It's hard to explain.

It's no good breathing through my mouth. If I do that, I can taste it. She's standing in the kitchen. She's spraying hairspray and looking at herself in a mirror that she's balanced on top of the microwave. She keeps adjusting little bits.

I can see my dad through the kitchen window. He's in the back garden smoking a cigarette. He's looking up at the sky. Maybe some trees too that pass through his vision. He stands there so often that sometimes when I look out the window it looks like something's missing if he isn't right there. I have to stop myself from trying to work out what he's thinking about because I know it'd be too much for me to handle on days like these. I think my dad feels like he's hardly been seen and his days are numbered, like he's a background prop in the film of his own life.

My dad's retired so it makes sense that he's at home. He's always here. My mother is usually at work, so it's a little weirder for her to be here than him. Today, she's taken the day off. I don't know why. They've already had breakfast. I can see the washing up and toast crumbs on the breadboard. It's something they still do together.

"Morning,"

"Morning."

Sssspppprraaayyyyyyyyy.

"How come you're not at work?"

"I've taken the morning off." And I think she said a little bit more after that. Reasons why. But I only followed enough to tell it didn't have much to do with me.

Yesterday was nothing. Today is the funeral.

I take a bowl from the cupboard. I fill it with cereal. I pour milk on the cereal. I sit down in the front room and close the door with my foot. I turn on the television.

A news channel is talking about a bombing in a country that I always get confused with other countries around it. It's hard to know what to think. A guy drove a bus filled with explosives into a building. He was a suicide bomber. It doesn't say what his name was, that probably went with him, as far as we're concerned. I think that it's a different place to where that bomb exploded the other night but if so, the newscasters aren't making any comparisons to the earlier one.

Alex called. My other best friend. Not today but last night. That's weird. I just found out. He spoke to my dad. My dad wrote "Alex called" on a Post-It note and put it down. It must have fell. Maybe it wasn't sticky enough. I just found it on the floor next to the table where we keep one of the telephones. I feel strange about the thing the other day, it feels like forever ago, the stuff to do with Alex and Luke's faces. I must have been totally stoned. It's so easy to get confused. As in it's easier than anything else. I guess if you stare too much at someone you know then they just start to look really different from what they were before and more like some other thing else you know.

I leave the television on and take the phone upstairs. I look up Alex's number on my mobile, and dial it on the house phone. It rings for a couple of minutes. It sounds scratchy. If Alex answers then it means I've woke him up.

"Uhh ... hello?"

"Alex?" I say that but I know it's him. His voice is always so dulled or something it's instantly noticeable.

"Hello?"

"How's it going?"

He coughs and then says: "Oh hey."

"How's it going? You called last night. Right?"

"Errr .... oh yeah. Umm. Hi. Yeah. Hang on a second." He's probably rubbing his eyes or sniffing or clearing his throat. I can imagine it real well. Clearing out blockages between him and me. After about ten seconds he's back.

"Yeah - I was calling to see if you were around. It feels like ages since I've seen you."

"Yeah. It does. It's been a while, haha." I don't know why I laughed. It felt like it was probably meant to cover a lot of stuff. Luke's dad is fucking dead.

"Ahh man. Haha. What time is it?" I picture Alex pushing his hair back. It looks greasy. I picture a red t-shirt too. Don't know why. It must fit the way I see him.

I look at the clock on my mobile phone: "Err ... it's 9:43am." I thought that would be funny. Alex doesn't laugh.

"Fuck."

"I know."

"It's early ... haha." So I guess it was funny.

"Did you know that Luke's dad died?"

"Shit. Yeah ... someone told me ... umm ... yeah ... someone said ..." He can't remember who. For about two seconds I feel insanely panicked about Alex's health. I carry on talking to change stuff.

"So you wanna hang out?"

"Yeah ... I've got some acid if you want to ... ?"

"Yeah. I think ... yeah. That might be cool. Umm ..."

"Ah great, man. Yeah. I mean ... that'd be awesome. It'd be good to see you."

"Yeah. When do you wanna ... ?"

"Um ... you wanna come round?"

"Yeah ... when? When's best?"

"Ummm ... I guess I wanna get some more sleep first ... haha ... but ... maybe tonight? Like nine or something? Maybe a little after. I should be up by then ... haha."

"Oh cool ... yeah ... that'd be great. I was gonna say ... because I have to umm ... I have to go to Luke's dad's funeral first.

"Oh shit - it's today? Fuck."

"Yeah, I know."

"Man. OK. Well ... Jesus ... say hey to Luke. Tell him round if he ... fuck ... I dunno man ... just give me a ring ok?"

"Ok, I'll do that. Cool."

I've only got one suit. Luckily, it's black. My parents g me about a year ago or something. They said it'd be useful for important occasions. I think this'll be the first time I w put the suit on without thinking too much. I'll have to start to the funeral soon.

"Oh. You know I could have ironed that for you." Th mother's way of saying I look scruffy. I tell her it's ok and w the conservatory to look for my wallet, which I think I mig left there last night somewhere.

I look at my dad. He's still in the garden. He's standing patio wearing a faded blue shirt and staring blankly into the ... distance maybe?... He's not wearing his glasses and he's s a cigarette. Occasionally he bounces gently up and down balls of his feet. It's just this thing he does. I think probably like a nervous twitch, a fidget of energy that has to go som I've seen him do it when he's in a room with a load of pec nobody is talking to him. His skin looks patchy and old. He notice me standing there and I don't say anything.

Sometimes I wonder what he thinks about. I don't d often. It feels impossible. Everyone is so fucking lonely. people lose their minds everyday or something.

Sometimes I think I'm like a mirror; a really flatter People look at me to see the parts of themselves that they

see and the parts that they want other people to see. When they talk to me, it's like they're checking themselves. Pouting or something, but less direct. I think people know that I want to see the best in them. I guess it's easy to work out what to say sometimes.

When me and Emma have kissed, it's like she's been kissing herself. I mean, I make her happy to be her. Luke can sometimes be *really* cold, so she doubts herself. Emma likes to think that she can be everything to everyone, or change into what whoever she's talking to wants her to be. It's something to do with hating herself. She says that she's very sure of who she is but that's not about her being self-confident. When we're both stoned and I'm crying and telling her I love her over and over again until the words sound like something else entirely, then I guess it sinks in or it starts to mean something. I can really start to see that she knows herself.

I can't get my head around the idea that everyone used to be children. Like some fat, mean guy I see in the supermarket that pushes his way past me – he used to be a kid. If I just watch and don't say anything then I can see it in anyone. It's so crazy it makes me feel like I'm becoming light-headed. I can still tell I'm who I used to be. With friends too, I guess it shows. It takes a couple of seconds sometimes, but most people still look at each other like kids, it's not just me. The way they move towards each other implies that they see it. I'm thinking about the fact that my dad used to be little.

***

Some kid grew up to kill a bird. Maybe, anyway, since the bird could have just died normally. Dying, after all, is normal. I just realised that again. Maybe I remembered, whatever difference that makes. How is it that birds die anyway? I picture the bird just plummeting out of the sky. Flapping its wings one second and then bashing onto a roof like a stone in the next. A total collapse in truth.

There are probably tons of dead birds stuck on the tops of flats and trees. From up high they might look like they're sleeping.

Some little boy never thought he'd be messing around with a dead bird one day. I never did, so no one else could have. I think that has to make sense.

Whoever it was that did this probably came down that street with friends. You wouldn't want to do that alone. There'd be no reason. They were showing off, I imagine, must have been drunk. If they'd been stoned they wouldn't have wanted to touch it. Someone did it as a joke.

"Haha."

"Look!"

"Haha!"

"Eeewww!"

I'm guessing.

If the bird is still there then I'll see it soon, in the next five minutes. I'm taking a longer route to the funeral because I wanted to see it.

When I get there, it's moved. It's at the bottom of a wall now. It's turned round and more of it is poking out of the cup than there was before. I think someone has probably kicked it. That or the wind. I wish I'd said something to Luke at the time about seeing it there. I can't bring it up now because it didn't involve him and compared to everything else, it will just seem too dumb.

I crouch down about a metre from the bird and then move closer. The eye *that* I can see is open. It looks like it could be almost alive again – in that same second, it looks almost unreal. Maybe that's why someone would want to kick it…

"Eew – look at that!"

"What the fuck is it?"

"It's a bird!"

"Is it dead?"

"Of course it's fucking dead! Look, watch this…"

I try looking at real life again; stuff that's happening now. Part of me wants to put a hand out and flip the bird over so that I can see the worms and the way that its feathers are covering blank bones and tiny bits of rotted flesh and shit. I don't though, because I think I'm scared to, or it just creeps me out thinking about the germs and the stuff that I don't know whether or not to expect underneath its broken body.

A woman walks past so I turn away from the bird and pretend to be doing my shoelaces. She gives me this look that I can't figure out exactly so I just stare at my feet and pretend to fiddle with a knot until she's gone. Then I remember that I'm crouching on the ground, wearing a suit.

If Craig saw the underside of the bird, I'd like to think it would fuck him up, at least just a little. It'd be comforting if it did. It would mean a lot to me and also show the world what kind of person he was. I mean, someone good. He'd get all jumpy and girly but just for a second. Then he'd stare at it sombrely the way that I'm doing.

The girls who wrote stuff under Craig's pictures have missed the point. Next time I'm on the computer I'll send him a message. I'll have to make sure I'm stoned enough.

The colours on the drinks cup have faded. Ran out onto the street. It rained a few nights before. I don't know about the bird. I didn't see it before. I feel weird about the suit for a second. No matter how much my mood changes, it stays the same. I look at the body. I've seen fast food a thousand times but inedible stuff is different. I don't know about birds. There are probably tiny differences that I don't pick up on. I mean, you could eat it if you had to, or if that was your thing. If I was a bird then I'd know the difference. I notice it with people. Their faces. Their bodies. The things that they do. Sometimes their personalities and stuff though I worry that I get mixed up and only see myself even when I'm comparing my flaws to the good in someone else.

I'm looking at each feather one by one, as best as I can. They're actually beautiful. They're all gracefully different. Some are grey, the others are purple, some of them are green and some of them are brown. Some are mixes with names that I don't know. The greys are my favourite. At the moment anyway. I think that without all the grey feathers, the others wouldn't glow so much or look quite as impressive. The grey bits are holding the rest together so it's not mess that makes no sense and doesn't go with itself. It's a design flaw that's impressive.

The corpse looks better because of what I think is on the other side of what I'm seeing. If there are maggots and flies and dried up blood in there then it'll feel different, at the moment I know, but I don't know at the moment, so the body still looks good.

The only thing I could use to find out for sure what's beneath there is a cigarette lighter. It's a purple one, with a flywheel, that I think I stole from Luke when I was in the car with him sometime driving from nowhere to nowhere. I picked it up without thinking or without noticing that I was thinking. I don't know if I'll need something bigger. There are sticks lying around and branches off some of the trees. They're dirty though and I don't want to get any smudges on the suit that might freak Luke out or distract him from the obvious when I get to the funeral.

I hold out the lighter and rub my fingers round it like I'm trying to work out what I'm holding rather than thinking about what I'm meant to be doing. My hand shakes and I rock a little bit where I'm crouching. I readjust my crouch a bit to make sure I don't topple over. I start noticing the sound of gravel moving each time my feet change position. The noises started before that but I didn't notice it then. I'm listening harder now which I think is because I'm nervous.

The boy's basketball would send the gravel everywhere. If my father's glasses fell in this gravel they'd get chipped. I think about what it would feel like to lie down on it, maybe if I was naked. I don't know whether it would be comfy or not. Or it might feel a little bad but in a kinda nice way like the other day when I bit an apple and it made my teeth bleed. I used to wait till my gums were bleeding and then eat salty crisps so I'd get little stings everywhere. I was so dumb.

I stop thinking about it and poke out the lighter. The corpse doesn't move. The feathers just look squashed until I pull my hand back. My shadow lends everything a different shade. I bring the lighter back to try and make things look how they did before. I squint to see if that makes any difference to anything.

A breeze makes the feathers ripple. Something makes me paranoid so I look up. There's no one there. I poke the bird again but this time without thinking as much about things. The corpse moves a bit more this time. I push the lighter harder so that almost of half of it now is sunk into the cup and tucked between it and the body. I wiggle it slightly and feel some slight give. I probably disturbed some rotten skin that I can't see.

I try to flick the lighter up so that the bird flips out but the way that I do it doesn't work. The bird just jostles a little and droops even deeper. I put my hand back in my pocket for a second. My fingers remind me that the joint I rolled is still waiting in there. That reassures me and I figure I may as well have a real look at the bird since I came all the way out here. Otherwise I'd be wasting my time.

I grab it quick enough not to get scared and yank it out and over. Once it's done there's more time to think, so, just like you'd expect, I lose my mind. The noises that the flies are making must have been muffled before. Now they're louder than anything else that's making noise in my brain. That, or everything has started to make the same noise at once and, inside and out, it's a chorus.

I look down and see there's dried blood on my hand. I panic and wipe it without thinking, so that it smudges my suit. I run my hand over it but it spreads out and stains worse. There's some other stuff in the centre of it, some yellowy cream goo. Whatever it is, it's on my suit now as well.

I stop trying to fix it, seeing as it only spreads wider. I push my hand against the wall to get the rest of the blood off. Most of it comes off but there's a stinky remainder. I rub my hands together to get the last few bits of it off and then have another useless go at my suit.

I'm still on time but the thing with the bird has freaked me out and I'm approaching fast as I draw up to the church. I'm not sure what it suggests about how I was feeling before but I definitely start to feel worse as I close the gap to the steeple.

Luke's dad wasn't religious, unless he kept it well hidden. It was hard to tell what he was thinking most of the time, as a matter of fact. Now Luke probably feels like he knows the little he did even less.

People are dressed in black because they think it's polite. Colours must mean distractions. There was a girl I was looking at on the internet once. She died but her profile was still on some website. I found her through Craig's page. Her friends left photographs of her funeral on her page. Pictures of themselves, looking ahead and stuff. They're teenagers so they can do things like that without being inappropriate. They haven't started pretending yet. I suppose she must have wanted bright colours. Perhaps she thought if it was a party then her friends might remember her as more exceptional than she had been in life. They're holding pink and green balloons, with tears in their eyes, and sort of smiling, like they aren't quite sure. Her main picture is her as seen from above. It's all Photoshopped in colours as well so I can't tell what her face really looked like.

I make out Emma. She looks restless or scared. She holds a cigarette in her hand and moves it around more than she actually smokes it.

If I could then I'd turn into her. I know it wouldn't be easy, that everyone has so much stuff going on that they don't understand, but I don't know ... somehow other people still manage to be amazing. It's probably wrong to say but I'd spend so much time with my body if I turned into Emma. That would mean that it was still my mind in there, I guess.

I can't see Luke anywhere. He must be inside.

He probably has to talk to everyone who has come to see his dad. He's probably sick of seeing the coffin. I've not seen it so I'm just guessing again. I want Luke to come outside but I'm also glad that he hasn't. I need to be on my own with Emma. She passes me the joint that I thought was a cigarette and, as I take a toke, I stare at a crisp packet that's stuck in some stinging nettles next to an old-looking grave. I sense it's old because I can't read the name on it. Emma says something that I don't take in as I should, but I catch enough of to work out that it doesn't need a reply. It was something really obvious about how sad this all is that she only said because we've not spoken yet.

At home, my dad's probably asleep by now. When my mom goes out of a day, he sits down in front of the television and passes right out. Sometimes he stays like that all day. When she gets home from work, it wakes him up. One time he left a tap on for six hours and the kitchen flooded. It's hard trying to work out exactly what it is that's made him end up like this. I think he thinks if he stays asleep long enough, whatever has happened will all bleed away. I think it's the same thing he thinks about when he stands in the garden and smokes all his cigarettes and looks up at the sky. He's sleeping at those moments too.

Emma takes the joint back and I blink to myself. She leans into me, so I put my arm round her and gently squeeze her shoulder. I try to pretend that I'm comfortable but can't seem to manage. I'm worried that someone might see us.

There's a dream that I had when I was four that I used to be able to remember so clearly that I'd get confused about whether the things that happened in it might have happened in real life. I was sitting in the house with my mom, my dad and my brother. We were all on the floor cross-legged, playing a board game, Hungry Hungry Hippos. We had to hit these brightly coloured plastic hippos as fast as we could so that they'd eat all of these plastic balls before anyone else could. Their balls were supposed to be food. I guess the purpose of the game was to try and make your friends starve. There was a painting on the wall that showed a man walking away from an old wooden house that had the look of a barn or a farm building. I think the picture was supposed to be of a hot summer's evening – the house and the man were black silhouettes and the sky was red, orange, pink. When I was younger I always used to think that the house was on fire. I thought that the man was either escaping from the blaze or it was him that had started the fire because he hated his family. He was carrying something over his shoulder. Then something happened to the painting. I can't remember what. Luke says that our memories aren't good anymore due to the drugs we've taken. Maybe with me that's the case, because his seems fine. Or maybe it isn't, I don't know anymore. I can't see into his memory but it always seem there. I wish almost more than anything that I'm in somewhere inside of it. Maybe what happened was the painting kept moving. But only the background like it was catching up with

61

the man. Something about the television was fucked up too. It flickered or something, or turned itself on and off. The only thing I remember for sure is us sitting there. The dream went for ages and we never got up, we just stayed in our place. All of this feels completely impossible

Emma's eyes seem reflective which means they look like glass. She's barely said a word since we first stood together. She and Luke might be much better off if it was me that was dead. I sometimes see her thinking that when she looks at my face. But then again it could actually be nothing.

"Hey." That was Luke's voice. He's found us at last. Neither of us answers but we know that he's there. We adjust our hug so that it faces him. For a second I think he might turn away without speaking, which would basically mean that everything is fucked, that there'll be no use to this day, but then he walks over and I pass him the joint.

He takes the last drag and flicks the butt into the stinging nettles that are cracking through the grave that has probably been around and hasn't been thought of forever. After that, the funeral starts.

We walk into the church. Luke moves to the front and sits next to his aunt. She's wearing a black hat. That's all I can see. Emma follows him even though it looks like Luke's ignoring her. I know that this is going to feel longer than it will actually take.

An old woman whose face makes me think of the bark on one

of the trees outside stands behind me and I panic about the dried dead bird's blood on my suit, so I sit down in the seat nearest to me, which puts me at the back of everything. I think about what Alex must have looked like when I spoke to him on the phone. I bet his eyes were bleary.

I miss a signal. People are standing up so I stand too. The church smells like damp wood. There's music and I can't begin to imagine from the sound what the person who wrote it must look like. I see the coffin and then it disappears. I see it again and then it's gone – back and forth as a man a few rows in front of me keeps moving his head around to get a better view. The same thing is happening with Emma. I catch glimpses of her when people fidget.

I try not to listen so that this whole thing just stops until it's over. It sounds like someone is making threats. The man at the front is talking about someone coming back to life, but not Luke's dad. Jesus, I guess. Or all of his disciples. The man is telling everyone that there's a way to live forever and something about choices. I'm sure that all of this isn't as important as it's pretending to be. Luke's dad being dead is important, but I think people have misunderstood why.

People sing. Normally Luke would laugh at this kind of thing. I can see Emma more clearly. She keeps turning her head to the side to see if Luke is looking at her. I guess he's not. She looks like she just saw someone die, but is pretending that she didn't. I'm so tense that I want to scream but don't even know what I'd cry out if I did.

I space out and start thinking about other things. If I was crying then it would be at the wrong things.

I know that the chequered pattern in the email that was only a joke actually stays still and tricks people into thinking there's been some type of movement. It seems like it might be related to paranoia in that respect, but that's just a feeling I have, where I'm sure of a plot, and there's nothing close enough to words that I could use to explain it.

The song ends and someone else starts speaking. I only start paying attention when Luke stands up. He reads a prayer that means nothing to him and that I think would mean nothing to his dad, either, so they have that in common. It means something to the other people though, unless they're pretending as well. Some of them, now I look at them, seem really upset. It must mean something to Emma because she's crying. Luke looks like he's going to faint for a second in this way that makes his skin go really pale. I want to kiss him − or for Emma to kiss him − and for me to be Emma or Luke to be me. When Luke finishes reading everyone sings again. I look at song lyrics on a photocopied programme and move my lips like the lyrics but make no sounds. No one will notice I'm not joining in. There are enough people making the noise so that I don't need to.

Some of the ceremony gets lost in a blur I try hard for. The joint did the rest. I taste catarrh and feel hotter than I should. I don't know if the body is on fire now or if that happens later. I decide as we file out that it doesn't matter.

I'm glad to be outside at last, stopped on the steps. Luke stands nearby and talks to the guests. He thanks them for coming again and again. Emma stands next to him but she doesn't say much. I can tell she's doesn't feel close enough to Luke to play the part of his family as people approach her. The hidden look on her face tells you she wants to be elsewhere. Still, her body's like a placard that announces she's there.

There's dried blood under my fingernails from scratching my suit. There's the patch where I've rubbed the blood in. I fold my arms so I can feel better covered *up*. Maybe it looks like I'm trying to deal with something, too. People nod at me like they're not brave enough to smile, or like I've done something wrong. I think I'm making this worse. People probably hardly notice me so I need to stop obsessing with thoughts that they are. I need less people to be here.

After awhile, Luke signals something in my direction which I guess means don't move. He says something to his aunt who nods in an "I understand" kind of way and self-consciously hugs him. He loosens his tie and walks over.

"Let's go for a walk," he says. Then he lets out this weird breath and at the same time says "FUCK!"

We follow him behind the church, down some path that goes up onto some grass under some trees. Everything is wrong and I don't get how it could ever realistically start getting right again. I might have known at some point but I think I assumed too much about people.

Emma is with us, trailing behind. I can't be sure if that's us or her choice. "What are you going to do with all the flowers?" she asks. Luke doesn't answer. She only asked that so we'd know she could talk to him.

"There are so many flowers." It's the same question again.

"My aunt said she'll tidy up." So he answers that time. He must have felt bad, by which I mean worse.

"Your house will smell nice." Emma looks like she might cry again, though not about Luke. It's more like she understands how pointless it is to talk the way she's talking to somebody like him.

"I'm just gonna take the lot of them to some accident scene. You know when cars crash and people leave flowers next to a smashed up lamppost? I'm gonna dump them all there. Trick someone's ghost into thinking they were more loved than they realised. Ha." Luke's laugh sounded more like a yell. I smile but try to make it look like it's painful. I'm only guessing what he wants.

For a second I get a buzz about something. Luke's dad is dead and I'm one of the only ones here. That must mean something significant. So what if we're not holding hands. Luke looks a little

65

more real. He stands under a tree and frowns at something. Emma watches him do it.

"Alex has got some acid." As soon as the words leave my mouth I feel stupid. I want the words to come back so I can swallow them down like the pill that they're mentioning. It's like they chose themselves to be said rather than me getting to think too much about saying them before they came out.

"What?" Luke says that. Then he starts laughing. Maybe I should feel happy because he's amused but I only feel bad. I don't know. I don't think Luke thinks what I said is funny in a good way. I mean, it was hardly meant to be funny in any way. It was just something to say that is true. It wasn't intended as an ironic statement about the condition of things. I only wanted him to know that I'm here for him.

Luke says that he needs to be alone and that he'll phone us later. I think we might meet up in the evening. Emma forces a hug out of him and he limply returns it. Then he leaves us standing together behind him.

"When did you speak to Alex?"

"This morning." It feels strange to talk to Emma about Alex. I think they might have slept together once, when Emma and Luke were still getting stuff together. It makes me feel too nervous thinking about it.

"How's he doing?" She means about drugs and stuff. I think people gave up on him because it was too scary.

"He sounded ok. He's got his hands on some acid."

"Yeah. What's he doing?" She means with his life.

"Umm ... I don't know. He sounded tired, I guess. He called me last night but I only got his message this morning so I rang him back. He sounded surprised. I guess not many people have been asking after him."

We walk without talking about too much else, or anything else that's important. Neither of us says it but I think we've both stayed together because we don't know what we could do with the rest of the day, particularly when it's one a funeral's been on. As we cross towards town, we stroll past a petrol station. I buy a sandwich and Emma buys a chocolate bar in a bright golden wrapper. It shimmers as she crinkles it back.

It's starting to rain. We stand underneath the porch of a newsagency, eating and waiting. Emma asks if I'm definitely going to go to Alex's later. I tell her that I don't know because I don't, and also because I think she might want to come with me if I do. I don't want her to come. I want to be with her all the time until we die but that's different. I don't want anyone else to be there with us, just us two. The rain sounds like bubbles popping.

I hold Emma's hand. She looks at me like I don't know something. She says that she should go home and leaves. I realise there isn't a bus due for another twenty minutes so I decide to walk home. The suit gets shinier and heavier as I move through the rain. The blood stain looks fresh-made and sticky.

My parent's car isn't on the drive when I get back, so I start taking off my clothes as I walk up the stairs. I dump them on the floor and turn on my computer. I send Craig a message telling him that I hope he doesn't mind a random email from a stranger but that I think I recognize him from somewhere and that if he ever needs to talk about anything then he can talk to me. I want to add that I know that when I was his age I thought that I may have hated life and even though I'm only a little bit older than him now, I know that things can get better – even though as I'm typing the message I know that they can't – and then I'd ask him to tell me about himself and try to make myself sound cool and like I'm not in love with him from afar and the idea of him and everything about him and that his beauty doesn't make me feel confused about everything and then I tell him that I'm stoned so that I have an excuse in case he thinks I sound dumb even though I *am* stoned and the rest and I try to ask questions that might give me a better idea about him as a person, I try to sound like I know what's happening in my life even though I haven't got a hope of doing anything interesting ever because I'm so terrified that my mind isn't right, which is the sign that isn't, and I don't tell him that every time that I've seen him I've felt like dying inside even though I don't understand why and that I think he means a lot of different things to me, so many in fact I can't make out what, and I write more things that I don't even think about and couldn't remember if I tried but I think they're weird scary things or just really upsetting things or just stupid things that make me sound like an idiot or worse and then I highlight everything I just wrote and look at how black the screen is with white-interiored words and then I un-highlight everything and the screen is white and the words *are* black again and then I highlight everything over so that the screen is black and the words *are* white but this time I put my finger on the delete button and think about dumping everything that I've done but I don't press the delete button, not just yet, I just leave my finger on it for a moment and I feel like I'm going to start burning alive if I stay like I do and I think a little more about Luke's dad but not long enough to actually realise that I'm thinking it because these thoughts all go so fast before they're carried away and then, as if in response to that notion , I make up my mind and click send.

I lay back on my bed and stare sideways at nothing.

The rain still sounds like bubbles popping.

68

6

One night we broke into a 24 hour petrol station that had been closed for about a year. There was a tear in the fence that had been wrapped around the property when the place went out of business, so we made it bigger and crawled through. We stayed there from about 11 at night till 2 in the morning. Luke sat on a skateboard and occasionally rolled across the forecourt, trying tricks that he couldn't really pull off. Emma and I watched him and passed a bottle of vodka that she had stolen from her dad back and forth between us till it was all gone and we left. The three of us lay about and just were with one another. It felt like the feedback that fades out the end of punk rock songs.

7

My brother is screaming at my dad. I think one of them threw something. My dad shouts back. Someone shuts a door so hard the stuff in my room shakes. I turn up the music so loud that I can't even hear the song properly. I mouth the words as hard as I can. Maybe I'm whispering a couple of them, but really forced and quiet. My throat hurts. This whole house feels like it's been dying so long the rot itself is impatient.

My mother had a coughing fit and is in her chair downstairs, epically panting. I think it's got something to do with the shouting but they don't admit it because they're trying to pretend that everything's fine really angrily.

I wish that music meant what it used to mean. If I could work out when it changed then I might be able to look at what I'd been doing and work out what I'd done wrong. I think it still sounds the same but I just don't feel as excited as I used to. Luke still listens to music, but I don't know what that means. He made me this CD. The headphones feel like they're holding my head in their hands and letting me cry against their chest even though they haven't been able to help me like they used to. The thing that kills me is that I'm trying so fucking hard and it's only barely the minimum.

I think about what my mum was like as a child. I can only guess. You have to work your way backwards to do that kind of thing and she seems like she's nothing but present. The fits make her seem old but when she starts shaking, she's not even that, she doesn't seem like anything apart from a body that isn't working properly with a wide-eyed head. When she was young I think that she was probably really happy for a while, and then when she started realising that the happy stuff doesn't work, when the people looking after kids don't try as hard, things started changing. When people get bored then stuff goes wrong, and once people start seeing sadness as the end to their boredom then it's pretty much over. I think that's how it works, even though something about the drums and the guitars and the guy screaming about making things better are trying to say something else.

The last time I kissed Emma I was so scared of Luke walking in that I had to stop and pretend that I'd realised something very important and talked about it instead. I think she kissed someone else after that and Luke saw and didn't care. I sat staring at him wondering if he knew how much like life he was to me and how bad I was afraid of him becoming.

In my room, I put the headphones on the floor because none of the words sound like anything but noise, the same as the shouting. I can't tell if that's stopped or not.

I call Alex but he doesn't answer which is fine because it's only four. When I look away from the computer my eyes are heavy like the sky wants me to look somewhere else, because it's realised that it's run out of everything at the moment. I check my profile three times in ten minutes to see if Craig has read my message. I try and find out if I can delete stuff that hasn't been read but I can't so I stare at his face and keep zooming in so that the flesh turns into blotches of bitmap that end up looking a bit like the puzzle someone sent me. I email them back and ask where they found it.

I watch a video of the dead actor where he says that falling in love made his films mean less. My internet connection is running slow. Stuff keeps stopping. His pigment pixelates like the computer's cremating him. It keeps pausing when he's half way through speaking like its secret wish is that it wants to be death.

The actor looks high, but I think everyone does anyway.

He fidgets. He can't sit still. He scratches his arms and jumps at questions really fast like he wishes he could drown in them. He drinks some water but keeps staring at whoever's behind the camera talking to him and then plays with the empty bottle like it's actually a stress ball. The little microphone on his shirt keeps picking up the scrunching plastic. When was the last time he slept?

The actor might be right. Not just because he's dead. I mean what he said about love. The more I've thought about Luke, the less I've listened to music. I can't remember which came first though and I think that it used to be fine so the actor could be wrong. All I know is that a lot of stuff is less important than it used to be when I wasn't in love and losing my mind like this. I push a folder of magazines onto the floor. I take the one that lands on top and start tearing it to pieces. I think I'm doing it because everything feels that way anyway.

My mum needs some special drink that she likes because she thinks that it helps her *to* feel better. She's run out, I hear her telling my dad through the wall. I volunteer to get it so that I can get out of the house. I say that through the wall too.

It takes ten minutes to walk to the supermarket. I go past the lake where kids throw bread to the ducks even though I heard an expert on the radio saying that it actually kills ducks to do that. The kids don't know and wouldn't understand. They seem okay not knowing they're murderers.

Outside the supermarket a man stands at a cash machine. I notice that he's trembling. He tries one card and presses buttons. The card comes back out and he wipes his face with his hand. He pulls another one from his pocket and tries that instead. The same beeping noises go off as if he's making it angry. His hand really shakes when he scratches his head. He reads something on the screen then shakes more.

I enter the store and walk past the books stacked just inside. All of the author's names are bigger on the cover than the names of their books. If I squint they look just like washing powder.

An old woman counts out her money on the counter of the cigarette kiosk. The man serving her looks impatient. He tries to smile but comes across tired. The closer I get the more unsettling the woman looks. She's tried to draw her eye brows on but hasn't done it too great; it makes her look like a cartoon character that's just been attacked. Her black wig has slipped to one side. Part of her scalp is showing and looks scabby, bald and red. The queue behind her gets longer but I guess she doesn't notice. The man serving her is called Carl. It says so on his badge. It also says I'm here to help you.

The supermarket makes me feel ill. The air is strange and the ceiling feels really low. The light is too artificial. There are these long fluorescent strip lights everywhere. They make my eyes ache, like something really mean and fake is weighing down on them from above. Supermarkets probably do that stuff on purpose so that people freak out and buy loads of stuff they don't need just so they can get out of there.

Everyone wants to sleepwalk their way through an advertisement.

My father sleepwalks. That's not a metaphor. He walks around while he's asleep. Apparently he's always done it – which makes me think about him doing it when he was a little boy *which he used to be*. The first time I saw it I was halfway through a nightmare. I was dreaming about something to do with anxiety because that's all that I can remember about the dream. I was still half asleep when I

73

opened my eyes and I guess there was some spillage from the dream into life and I saw something that looked like a blur of friends and fear and something else dancing and staggering across my bedroom floor. My father was a silhouette which made things worse. He was actually stood still so I made it up he was moving. The door hitting the wall was what woke me. I didn't know what was going on so I screamed at him to get out. I asked what he was doing and he said that he had been watching me sleep to make sure that I was ok. He went back out again.

It's crazy how my dad hasn't fallen down the stairs. He's pissed on the floor a couple of times. My mom has found him sitting *downstairs* on the floor not knowing how he got there or what's been going on. It's similar to how he is when he's drunk.

When my dad can't think of stuff to say he says that things are clever. I know he doesn't mean it. When he uses the word "clever" it's mainly because he doesn't want to have to think about other words he might use. My dad thinks that supermarkets are clever. When he has nothing to do and it starts to damage him he sometimes drives to supermarkets that he hasn't been to before, probably hoping he'll find something there to distract him.

My dad told me about one supermarket that was quite far out of town. It took him an hour and a half to get there. Stuff must have been really bad. When he told me about the new supermarket that he went to – although he didn't tell me that it was only because of death that he went there – he'd say something and then say "you wouldn't believe it", like the things that he was telling me about the supermarket were really big surprises.

"You wouldn't believe it."

I did believe it. I believed every word he said about the new supermarket before he finished saying them.

The thing that my dad said was clever about this supermarket was that it had two levels. There was an escalator that took people up to another floor, where there was a whole other region to buy stuff.

"It was huge!" he said and showed me with his hands. His face crumpled a little and his fingers made these strange pirouettes like he was trying to read Braille. " I mean, sure, ok, it's got the same stuff as here. But the place is just so big. You wouldn't believe it!"

I read somewhere that microwave meals make people depressed. It's probably how the steam rises out of them.

The supermarket lights and the fluorescent air are quickly beginning to get to me. So many people who used to go to my school or who go there now and have part time jobs work in this place. It's like a class convened off hours.

The guy who sold me and Luke our first weed pushes trolleys around outside, like he's the rattle of a big metal snake slithering its way around the parking lot. Whenever I see him he shakes my hand and he gives me this nod like I still might believe he's this tough gangster type that we tried to fool ourselves into believing that he was when he was in school. I'm sure he used to just sell us potpourri anyway mixed with a pinch of cannabis. I'd still pretend to be stoned because it was something to do and it made Luke laugh. I could never tell if he was feeling the effects or getting high off my pretending.

A middle aged man bashes his trolley into me. It thumps against my foot and rolls up and over it, which hurts more than I would have thought if I'd been told by someone else about it. I apologize even though it never would have happened if he's been looking where he was headed. He tuts like my apology changed the past and put me in the wrong. I scowl, mainly at myself for knowing that it won't do anything.

I find the drink that my mother thinks will help her feel better and go to the checkout. A woman drops some cans on the floor and

I bend to help her pick them up but the look she gives me makes me wish that I hadn't. I can feel my body heating up and sweat forming under my clothes and on my face. The place sounds like what space would if someone took away the stars. I wait in line for the okay to get out of here.

✳

Outside the shop the air feels cooler and less hurried so I try to make the most of it and head towards the lake.

An old man spots me sitting down when I get there and I know straight away that he'll come over and talk to me. He stands with his hands clasped behind his back and his chest puffed out like he's trying to look proud. The way that generation tend to. The man looks round a couple of times. The second time he nods at me. He sits down beside me which irritates me a bit because I came here to smoke a joint before I went home.

"See all those plastic rings there." He points at floating plastic in the water, the stuff that holds multi-packs of coke cans together. We used to get warned in school that we had to cut them otherwise ducks and swans would get their necks caught in them.

"You have to slit those things." I don't tell him that I already know because I don't want to talk to him. "Otherwise animals get throttled with them."

I think about a swan choking itself to death.

The guy barely seems real. It's everything someone acting as an old man would say. Someone fed him his lines. It's too much to think about. I think about uncomfortable scraping, feathers being parted, pink necks being rubbed and split.

The old man says something about his dead wife. It changes his mood. He's trying to be happier. He tells me that he got a jokebook. He tells me that he's got twenty jokebooks. I guess he didn't know how else to cope. He says he can retell about a hundred jokes. He tells me some that I get but aren't funny and some that I barely take in because I'm trying so hard not to breakdown in a mess. He says he gets on much better with younger people. He says he used to have a lad that would come round and visit him. He met him after his wife had died. He used to take the lad to car boot sales and cook him Sunday lunch and buy him trainers. He leans over too much and smells of whatever menthol sweets he's slurping. He said he was going to take the lad on holiday but something went wrong and the lad made up lies about him and caused too much trouble. The old man looks back at the lake. I think we both realise that there's not much point me sitting there anymore and I leave without saying anything.

If my photo had been on my profile then I would be worrying more than I am about the email I sent to Craig. The fact that a photo of me isn't attached on there calms me down a little. It assures me at least something is still maybe within my command.

The things he wrote on his page look rushed. There's hardly anything there. I can only base him on people that I've known or got the impression that I knew. I think Craig hates school. He probably doesn't talk to many people but when he does, it's quiet and funny and sharp or whatever. That's how I see him.

My parents spend so much time looking at holiday brochures. They go away a lot. They sit around at home looking for places to go and then they go there and it's just a new place to sit around and read English newspapers. All the foreign places they go have been turned into the same place.

One day my mother said something to me from the other room. I was sitting at the family computer trying to fix something I barely understood but was able to sort out because I recognized all the warnings that kept flashing up and followed the prompts accordingly. She said, "It's so still." At the time I couldn't tell if she was talking about the hot weather or everything around her. I didn't answer because she was talking to me.

I get home and walk in by the garage door. As I walk through the garage, my father comes past me, his posture really stiff like he's hiding something in his hand. I don't bother to doubt and ask him what it is.

"A bottle," he says in a voice that's half sarcastic and half trying to sound normal, which you could call defensive. I guess he feels hurt but more by himself. He screws the top back on and turns away while he does it.

I don't ask why he was trying to hide it when it's no secret to anyone because I guess I know and so does anyone. He picks up his car keys.

"You shouldn't drink and drive." That felt relevant.

"I'm ok." He's trying to sound so normal that it actually sounds ridiculously fake, like a clown hat he's wearing. "I need to go and pick something up."

"What are you getting?"

"Just some cigarettes."

"You shouldn't drink and drive."

"I'm fine."

He looks older than I've ever seen him look in my life.

I shrug, walk through to where my mother is now sitting and give her the drink she wanted. My brother has gone out somewhere. I hear my dad pull off the drive.

Emma's online. I hover above a picture of her that she took from above even though she didn't need to because she looks pretty without silly angles. I think about sending her an instant message to see if she wants to talk. There's a little icon telling me that I can. I wonder if she's already talking to someone and who that would be. I build these amazingly paranoid castles out of nonmaterial bricks.

Craig still hasn't read my message. He hasn't logged on today. There's a new comment underneath one of his pictures from a girl who is probably trying not to say how much his beauty makes her want to disappear from the face of the earth. I click on his picture so that it grows bigger. I try to pretend that I'm in line with whatever the depicted Craig's looking at. It's hard, though, to do that, not knowing what it is that I want to replace.

The internet feels like a hundred million voices getting lost in the ocean they make. I look at how loose Craig's clothes look. They're not baggy, but they just sort of hang there. He's got this grey t-shirt on that makes his arms look healthier than they might actually be or else it just blurs things. His arms could fit inside the sleeves twice over. There'd be no more room and it they might stretch but he could do it if he wanted to. I've no idea what he wants.

Emma's at her dad's house, which is where she lives when she decides that she's not getting enough or too much of whatever it is she gets at her mom's place. I should probably say that this is all just a daydream – although that seems like it's less important than it should be. She lays on her front with her legs from the knees down waving in the air as she types. She's writing an email to someone but my mind can't see, or doesn't want to think about who that might be, just yet.

She gets up and fetches a glass of water. She drinks it in a different room to the computer. Her dad's at work. She switches a fan on because her dad will complain if the house smells of smoke when he gets in. She lights a cigarette and sits on a swivel chair that her dad usually keeps at his computer. I can tell from the way that she blows the smoke out of the mouth and through an open window that she's thinking about Luke. I know she won't call him because Emma gets so fucking weird when she doesn't think that people are in love with her that it's predictable. She maybe looks at the phone but doesn't even think of calling him. It's a kind of punishment, she tells herself. I could be wrong, because I'm so fucked up at the moment, and so I'm pretending that everyone else does stupid things the exact way that I do. Either way I'm glad I don't have to consider it.

There's a couple of shiny helium balloons, made from cheap and thin plastic, floating around in the corner of one of the rooms (I can't decide which). They're from some clients of Emma's dad. He won a big court case for a lot of money, I think. The balloons are attached to a big rectangular gift bag. The bag looks like it had something expensive in it but is empty now. The balloon says THANK YOU on it, really life-size, large. A breeze knocks the balloons around so they gently bounce off each other like sleepwalkers trying to box.

Emma takes a pair of really clean looking scissors with red handles from out of a pot. She snips a purple ribbon. The balloons hop up to the top of the room and stay there, floating on their sides against the ceiling.

Being up there, they do nothing.

Emma has another drink of water. It's hot. This time she does it differently. She pretends she's in a film, or I do. There are lots of cuts and different camera angles and lighting in my mind. She, or I, focuses on the tap. A close-up. The silver of the tap wobbling through the lens of the water. The sound of the water battering on the white ceramic sink.

I think of something else that I can't decide so I stop.

The balloons are just there. That's it. Nothing else.

Emma walks into another room. This time I know it's her bedroom. She's back at the computer, looking at books she might order. She reads so much but never talks about it. Maybe she orders another one for herself.

If she's still got the same posters on the wall that she had last time I was there then she stares at one of them because it makes her think of being happy and getting wasted on the way to seeing a band that we all pretended to care a lot more about at the time than we actually did. She pulls her laptop lid down until it makes a clicking sound. She picks it up and puts it at a desk that's covered with bits of paper that she's hoarded. Pink Post-it notes and small torn open envelopes with letters inside. I wrote Emma a letter once but it was so fucked up and diluted or whatever by the song lyrics I tried to fit in to it to prove that I wasn't lying about the tiniest things I was saying that I don't think it made much sense. She probably kept it though, although I can't locate it on her imaginary desk.

She closes the door to her room and flops back onto her bed and thinks for a while. I wonder if when she thinks about Luke's dad burning up it looks different to the way that I see it. She's fucked Luke in that bed. I don't think about that because I've thought about it too much anyway.

I can't remember if I made her finish the cigarette so I put it back in her hand. The smoke makes all these shapes that you can see through.

81

I wonder now whether Emma is online so that she can talk with Alex. That would freak me out. I don't know if I'd be able to do the acid if Emma was going to take it too, because I always have this fear when I'm drugs that I might lose all the things that stop me from telling people the truth. Like sense. I don't know if Emma would take the acid anyway, I don't know if she's taken it before, but I can kinda see how she would have. Maybe she and Luke have done it in those times that I've not been with them and, for me, they haven't existed.

" Luke?"

"Oh hey."

"I know that you probably didn't need anyone phoning you but –"

"Oh no, it's cool. Listen, sorry if I've not been too with it you know?"

"Oh it's cool – I mean, listen, I know – it's ok." I probably sound so eager just because he's talking to me normally like he did when he used to.

"I just needed to go for a walk. In the end I just ended up walking home. We had the wake. I was planning on missing it, but I went anyway."

"How was it?" The question came out without much thinking.

"Oh ... ha ... fine ... people repeating themselves and ..." He trails off like he's just spotted something in the distance.

"Yeah. Dumb question."

"No, it's ok. I mean, I wouldn't know what to say to me either. I don't know what to say to myself."

"Do you know where Emma is?"

"No. Well, she's online, I mean. So probably at home. It says she's online."

"Oh ok. I should call her soon. I dunno. Did she say anything after the funeral?"

"Like what?"

"I dunno, I mean. I feel bad for being a dick."

"You haven't been. It's just all fucked up at the moment − you know − everything."

"Yeah."

"Oh, so I was meaning to ask ..."

"Yeah?"

"I mean, it's dumb but are you doing anything tonight?"

"No. My aunt is still here. She's staying here for a while. I dunno − it's nice of her to ... but you know ... no ... Sorry − no, I'm not − why?"

"I spoke to Alex."

"Shit."

"Yeah."

"How is he?"

"I dunno. I mean, he sounded ok." I can't remember if he did or not but Luke isn't really asking so maybe that isn't a lie. "So, the acid. I mean ..."

"Fuck. Yeah − you mentioned it.." before but it kinda didn't go in properly."

I feel bad for suggesting it. I don't say anything because I'm trying to work out what "fuck" actually means when it's said in the way that it just was.

"Yeah. Whatever. I'll come." I guess Luke just wants to have a go at pretending to be stable for the night and see if it's a possibility for the future or something. I hope it doesn't seem worthless.

"Are you sure? I don't wanna ... " Words wouldn't work for this one without sounding like something from TV, so I stop. People know how conversations work anyway. I feel a buzz just from Luke contemplating being himself.

"Yeah. I don't know about the acid. I want to get out though."

"Yeah."

"I could drive us if that's easier?"

"Yeah, cool." Luke gives me a time and we both agree.

"OK bye." I listen to his voice get moved along by the speaker touching against the receiver which gets moved along to the dialling tone that started the whole thing and then to my listening ear, which for some reason is still on the phone, listening to the disconnection return here.

In my daydream the balloon is still on the ceiling. I don't know how much air it's lost. I guess it never has to lose any if I don't want it to.

Luke won't look anything like he did at the funeral. I'm listening to his CD again. It feels like an earthquake I'm watching on TV. I guess my dad's buying booze somewhere. I want to see Luke laugh a little bit.

I don't know what lies the man at the lake had told about himself.

In my head, Emma is still on the bed. I've taken the pictures off the wall and made everything white so that it's like a cube. Like if someone took a square out of the e-mail's chequered pattern. Or a sculpture of a hollowed-out sugarcube. One time, Emma showed me this artist on her computer who only made art using big white cubes. So the artist would fill a room completely with them, or stack them one on top of the other so that they'd make a wall. The artist would build these really huge walls, then, that were so high that you couldn't see over them, though I'm guessing if you could there would just be more white cubes inside them, protected I guess. Emma explained to me why the artist was so great. I can't remember what she said now because I think I was stoned and her words seemed too soft to lodge or something, like they needed to be sharper to prick me or firmer so I could hold onto them. I remember just thinking that the cubes would probably be really good to touch.

I think about what it would be like if Craig was there with Emma. He wouldn't know what to do, I guess. I try a few different things but settle on Craig lying on his back with Emma sitting on his stomach. They're both naked. She's rubbing herself back and forth on his stomach so that it kinda glistens or looks different depending on the light. Craig's just looking up at Emma, looking kinda nervous but peaceful. Wired too. And a little like God. Less so than Emma. No, wait, I can't tell. God keeps swapping. She's looking down now and loving how his eyes are taking her in.

Craig's jeans are on the floor inside out on top of his scuffed trainers. They're made by a skateboard brand, but I can't remember him skating.

Emma's sitting on Craig's dick and riding slowly back and forth, leaning back on her left arm which is rested on one of Craig's legs to keep her balanced. Craig's legs are stretched out in a straight line and his toes are twitching round like crazy. His arms are straight by his side. He's looking up at her, staring at the way that her body changes shape as she moves, looking at her eyes and the confident thrilled grin that she's shining down at him.

Craig hasn't read my message but his picture is on my computer screen which I think is enough. Him sitting, staring. I open a picture of Emma from her page which I go on more than she thinks and make it smaller so that I can fit on the screen next to Craig and keep swapping my eyes between the two.

I try changing things again so that Craig is actually really good and Emma's on her hands and knees and they're both moaning like they're dying or something. I imagine it being really hot but really fresh too which can't happen but I'm trying to imagine ideal situations, so I guess the impossibility of stuff is irrelevant.

Emma's back on Craig's stomach, wiping her pussy over his belly. She's got her arm back behind her, playing with his dick, pulling it up and down. I don't know whether it's fast or slow. I think a lot about Craig with his eyes closed. Maybe his head tilted back a little bit, too. I swap Craig around a couple of times, shuffle him so that he's Luke and then some boy I've seen in the street, and then another boy from school looking how he did when he was twelve and then Emma's dad but I stick with Craig because it seems like there should be some kind of ... loyalty? ... to this thing.

I never like to be in these things myself. My own image would blur stuff incredibly. It seems clearer if it's other people there, enjoying themselves. I can be the hidden benefactor of everyone this way. I can also slot myself into them. I take turns at being Emma's hips and Craig's hands. I think so much that I almost forget what anybody looks like when I become the combination of their thighs.

I'm trying to work out what I'm getting at. Their bodies are just hints, I think. Emma's tits squash and press against Craig's chest. He's gripping the sheets with one hand and holding onto Emma's back with the other, but flatly, loose, in a really noncommittal way. They're putting their heads together and I realise that this is the first time they've been kissing. It's hard and Emma's head jolts up and down a little bit. Craig's face is like clay at the various stages of being shaped. Sometimes I feel like everything is already lost. Still no clue as to what I don't understand; like the sex isn't enough, but

86

it's the closest alternative to insight or something.

Emma liked the effect that the white cubes had on the space around them, I think. Yeah, I remember that much.

So now Craig's on his knees and he's grabbing around in between Emma's legs. She's sitting on the bed looking down and occasionally casting her eyes up at the ceiling which is different to the one where the balloon is floating. She breathes heavily into the air. I guess I've given Craig more confidence than he had? He's licking and tickling and sucking and all sorts of things that I'm making vague as I watch them. The focus is more on Craig's back. It's so complex. I make things clumsy too, because that's how it would be.

In the photo of Emma she's pulling a silly face that's still really sexy because her lips are this strained colour and her skin is flushed like she's been running in the cold.

I can still tell that neither of them is close enough to realising what I want. They both need to be matching parts of the same person or something for the effect to work. But I don't want it to be a romantic thing.

I stop everything because Craig has read my message. I don't know how I feel. Not as worried as I was before. I guess that with Luke wanting to get back to normal it puts other stuff in the same optimistic buzz.

Craig must be so lost, but I don't know how I know it. He'll find something in my email anyway. It'll mean more than people just telling him that he's beautiful, because that stuff must just seem like clouds of smoke constantly disappearing or something, or being blown in his face, or something else that doesn't explain anything and is out of my reach. Fuck it. He's read the message anyway. I want him to feel like he must be someone special for me to tell him all the things that I did. Because he is.

Emma stands up and looks at herself in the mirror. I think about it more seriously and am confused with what I come up with. I want to be able to know everything about her, and for her to know me. I want both of us to be holding each other and crying, knowing nobody else matters. Though that'll probably change. Emma holds a telephone and dials a number. Mine.

I cum and nothing happens.

8

If I ever committed suicide, then I'd do it by drowning myself. I decided that a long time ago, I can't remember when. I have this idea that it might be a beautiful way to die, or at least the most beautiful way out of the options I could think of; although I'm probably wrong because I get mixed up when I'm trying to work out when things are special or not. Maybe it's actually a really horrible way to die. Maybe when you drown your lungs burst or cave in or bloat against themselves. I don't know. Maybe I should look into it, although I should probably just leave it. I've tested myself a couple of times. I've held my head under the water in the bath just long enough for the world to start tingling. It didn't take long for my head to burst out, splashing and soaking the bathroom floor. More and more when the thought of drowning comes to me, I think about the sea, which sounds a lot more obvious than it feels in the moment. The hard part would be fighting the urge to get out of the water. I'd have to force myself not to react. If I ever happen to hurt myself, then sometimes if I think about nothing but the pain and stop trying to get away from it then it can actually feel really good. It sounds fucked but it's true. Like there's a lantern inside of it. So I guess drowning would be the same if I thought hard enough about the pain I was feeling. It'd be like being told what to do by somebody that knows what they're doing.

9

"To tell you the truth I don't think I've really missed anybody." That's Alex. He looks like an animal, although probably a really cute one that would drive people crazy. Maybe like a Manga version of a racoon, a stoned one. He looks nothing like Luke.

"I mean the thing is…" He stops to search around on the floor for something ... a lighter. "I think that once you've got used to your own company – I'm putting that wrong – I mean, if you can really get on with yourself when you're on your own, then you won't have as many problems, I guess. That's how I think about it, you know?"

"Yeah." I keep getting distracted by how tired he looks. Or just how pale he is. Again, plenty of people would love it. Alex probably shows how fucked up a lot of people are. He looks like how magazines would try to make kids our age look although he smells worse, or his place does – not bad, but just like it needs more air.

"Shit. Man. I'm sorry about your dad." That was to Luke, who's just taken a joint that I passed him, a thing which seems so familiar that I have to try not to smile.

"Yeah. Let's not talk about that anyway. Death is boring." Everyone does this laugh that doesn't go too far from where it started.

"How have you been man?" Alex means me.

"Uhh ..." I think that's the sound I make. Close enough. "I'm ok." For a minute Alex looks at me and I can't tell if he's trying to read my mind rather than trust my words, but either way he's polite, or maybe just doesn't notice that I'm uncomfortable and carries on saying what he was saying.

"How's Emma?" Part of me feels like I should be answering that question but I leave it to Luke, who seems to handle things well.

"She's ok."

"I was wondering whether she was gonna come over, too ..."

"No. I didn't really tell her that we were – I mean not for any reason or any... I don't know. Things are weird."

Luke just nods like the last three words explain a lot. To me it felt like I don't know what. I want to see things how Luke sees them, maybe just at this second anyway, so I know what is weird about him and Emma. I don't ask because they're already talking about something else – someone who I don't think I know – and I wouldn't want either of them to know how lost I'm getting in the most straightforward things.

"Haha, sorry – do you want a drink or anything?" Alex walks out of the room and Luke asks for whatever there is and I do the same.

The place is a wreck. The carpets are covered with lots of little bits. Crumbs and other stuff. Lots of empty cans and plastic drinks bottles. Some of the cans have the last bits of cigarettes sitting on top, where they've been used as ashtrays. There are lots of mugs lying around, all dirty; Alex walks back in and takes a couple of them. He leaves the room and we hear water.

I roll another joint while Luke skims through the pages of a book that's been lying on the floor and that I was going to lean on to roll the joint if I hadn't found an empty CD case on the floor closer to me. There's a big crack running down the middle of the case I try to prevent the weed rolling into.

The book Luke's looking at is about ghosts. I wonder whether he's thinking about his dad. Maybe he doesn't think of ghosts and his dad at the same time yet. Maybe the ghosts in the book are more like a cartoon version of ghosts, though that'd probably bring them closer to his dad. He turns a few pages really fast and every now and then he bends the spine of the book and leans forward a little bit like he's really concentrating on what he sees, but it's hard to know if he is. I think about what Craig has written back to me if he has and what it might say. Maybe right now I'm like a ghost to Craig. I might add a picture to my page.

This must be like morning to Alex. He seems like he's still waking up. He gives me a glass that's wet from just being rinsed but still has smudges around the rim. I take it though, because I can tell it's the best I'm going to get. It's filled with wine — red. Luke gets given a mug with a comic book character slowly fading from the side of it. I think there's a chip in it because Luke turns it round and drinks from the other side.

"Thanks man." I just passed Luke the newly lit joint. He puts on the TV, which lights up the room, and passes the controller to Alex. Alex pulls this face at the TV like it's a mystery to him or he's really unimpressed. He changes the channel.

We're watching a man standing in front of a house. It's in America. I don't know which part. The man's standing in front of the house with a microphone. He's the presenter. It's hard to tell how tall he is when he's on TV. His suit looks expensive.

The programme cuts, so that we can see inside the house. I forgot to say that the outside was painted white and it looked like it was made of wood. There are two men sitting at a table eating breakfast cereal. They're wearing identical clothes and they look strange. They appear about forty. They're twins.

The presenter is talking about the two men. It's just his voice. *I* remember reading how TV tricked people; like in some horror films when people hear the sound of someone's brain being lobotomised or something horrible, the sound was actually made from a man squishing up a pumpkin in a totally different building, weeks after the video was done. But when they're put together it's the same thing. I think about what they'd use to make the plastic scraping on the swans neck which makes me think about the bird which I was hoping I wouldn't have to because it still feels really raw when I do.

The presenter is back on the screen and he's sitting on some cheap looking settee with the two men, who are showing him some paper with lots of scribbling on it; theirs, I think. The camera cuts again and shows a close up of the paper. It's a list or lots of lists

92

together; they look like they were written really fast. The men both have matching caps on with some logo that I don't recognise. I think it's the logo of a theme park. There's a picture of a log flume on it.

"They're savants." That was Alex. He's seen the show before, probably when he was fucked up on his own, which could be anytime. "They remember stuff, like insane details really easily. Like they could tell you every single thing about their favourite TV show, but I mean *every* single little detail like all the different clothes that their favourite character has worn in the entire history of the show or something. It's crazy."

"But they're retarded?"

"Well, yeah."

The camera cuts but everyone is still in the same room. The presenter is asking the savants questions. He's testing them, asking them about their favourite TV programme, some long running quiz show. The savants are getting every answer right. They answer so fast it's almost like they've learnt all the questions beforehand, which I guess they have, but over twenty years or something.

"When was the first episode of the show aired?"

"July 28th 1986." They both answer at the same time, I think. Their voices sound really nasal and shaky.

"Haha, wow." The presenter's teeth are so white his skin looks like suntanned leather. "And I bet you could even tell me what day of the week that was couldn't you?"

"Monday."

"That's incredible – wow!"

The presenter carries on testing the men but the sound changes back to the voiceover. It's the presenter's voice on its own talking about who has to care for the twins. It cuts to some really old people sitting in a different room.

The elderly couple are the twins' parents. They're worried about what will happen to the twins when there's no one left to look after them. The parents mean that they're going to die soon. The old mum puts her hand on the old dad's knee and says something like "We know we're not going to be around forever" which is strangely more emotional than I'd prepared myself to think.

I look up to see how the other two are dealing with things but Luke's got bored and is flicking through the book about ghosts again, and Alex is just frowning at the screen. He doesn't look sad.

The presenter just asked the savants if he was their favourite television personality. They said no. They said it really bluntly, but it was just because they were answering the question rather than trying to be mean. The presenter laughs like he would at children.

As a surprise, the presenter tells the savants that they are going to go and meet their favourite TV presenter, the one who presents the quiz show that they've been watching for years. They look really happy but kind muted as well, like it's both what they've always wanted and deeply besides the point. They both move around on the spot a little bit with their arms straight by their side rather than waving them around or something. They kind bounce a little bit on their toes. They make this strange sound and shake each other's hands really firmly which I'm guessing is their code for congratulations or something.

The camera cuts straight to a shot of the savants getting on a plane. There's a split second where the airhostess showing them to their seats looks at the camera or someone behind the camera with a nervous grin like she doesn't know how to behave around the twins but it's gone within a flash because I guess she doesn't want to look like she's uncomfortable or prejudiced at their condition, which the announcer has helpfully pointed out isn't technically a handicap anyway. There was probably at least a week or two in between the savants finding out that they were going to fly and them actually getting on the plane. But for us watching it was seconds. I think about how they would have been while they were waiting. Maybe the excitement was jarring for them or it made them too nervous. The presenter said something about them being really strict with routines and getting really stressed when things got changed around from what they were used to. So maybe in some ways flying into the sky felt like hell.

I notice a deep cut along Alex's arm. It's a sore, red gash that's scabbed over but doesn't look like it's healed properly. He might not even remember how it happened. I think about whether or not he fucked Emma. I could see how she would want to. I used to think Alex was really amazing until ... I don't know what stopped that, actually...

The savants are in front of a big metal gate and an orangey-brown brick wall. Someone, probably from the camera crew, says something into a little black box at the side of the gate and everyone waits for a second. A shiny sound voice comes back all crackled by the speaker and says "Hey! Come right in!" That voice must be the savants' favourite game show host because it sounds too brassy to be anyone else. The gates start to open. I think part of them must be scraping against the ground what with the straining noise they're making.

The pathway that leads from the game show host's gate to his mansion looks really long. It's in the middle of a big lawn that comes over so green it appears like it must have been done with paint or a computer. Actually, the whole place looks like a level from a computer game because it's so bright and leads somewhere else.

Luke is watching again now.

The game show host appears on a golf cart. He gets off and the savants shake his hand and stand staring at each other like they can't believe what's happening, which is a like a more pronounced version of how they always look, and then they get on the golf cart and the game show hosts starts driving them back to his mansion. The presenter says something about it being a dream come true and then it cuts to something else that I don't get to see because Alex changes the channel and dumps the remote on the floor.

"One of them dies."

"No way?" That was Luke. "That's depressing."

The wine that Alex gave me tastes like it's stale, but I like it anyway. Luke is on his second glass already. The bottle is near his chair. Alex is staring at the ingredients on the back of a can that he's just patted the embers of a cigarette into. I look at his fingers and think about how many things his hands must have done since I saw him last. It's not infinite, obviously, but it's hard to think of a number.

I think: If you say a word out loud over and over again, it starts to sound like something different that you've never said before.

Something on television makes Luke and Alex start talking about the dead actor. Alex says that he was into drugs. He says that he can just tell, but part of me thinks that he'll see drugs in anything. There's a rumour that the actor might have been gay and he killed himself because he was worried that people were going to find out. Maybe it was both things. Or maybe I think more about the gay thing because of the things I see in stuff. Maybe he just died. People die.

"I don't think he was gay," says Alex. I must have said something out loud which freaks me out because I didn't realise I had.

"Why not?"

"Have you seen the women he's been with? And his wife? Was he married? That girl, anyway. You couldn't you know ... haha ... you wouldn't want to lie about that, you know? I mean – Emma – haha – Luke – if you're with Emma, you're not gonna sleep with someone of the same sex, right? Ha."

I can't look at Luke because I can't handle whatever his response is. It'd make me think too much about things that have and haven't and have nearly happened, all of which amount to the same.

About an hour goes past and I start to wonder whether we'll actually get to take the acid because nobody has mentioned it yet. I don't ask, though, because even if it isn't, it'll sound like it's the only reason that I came to hang out with Alex. Maybe it is mostly the reason at this moment but it's not the only one. Still, I guess he's just enjoying having company. I dunno, I keep thinking that he hasn't seen people for months, but maybe he just hasn't seen me.

Before long, a guy turns up who Alex introduces to us. He's got a foreign name but I mishear it and by the time I've finished trying to unscramble that point in my memory, it seems too rude to ask. He seems ok but I find it so hard to relax around new people, all I really hope is that he isn't staying to do the acid because that might ruin the point of it and put me on edge.

I don't know if Emma knows that we're here. If Alex wasn't here then I think I'd want her here. If it was just her, Luke and me then that could be kinda beautiful. If the acid helped shine a torch on this bond that I've always hoped we had, you know, that would be amazing. Because when I think about the two of them ... I mean ... equally ... they're just ... They mean everything. I can't plot Alex in that.

I think the new guy whose name I don't know asks me something, which I only realise after Luke answers for me, and the two of them start talking about something that I'm still daydreaming on top of. The new guy is perched on the front of his chair and he's still holding onto the strap of a back pack that he was carrying that's now next to his feet.

"So what's going on tonight? What are you guys doing?"

Alex answers and says something about the three of us just hanging out and catching up and doesn't mention the acid.

It's stupid but I think part of me secretly prefers things that lack endings. I do things that I know will have no real finish to them. Like last summer I started emailing a random guy who lives near me. I made a fake profile on some sex website because it felt hot at the time. I didn't put a picture on it. I just put my age as being about eight years older and a couple of made up details that were so made up I didn't even think about them, hair colour and things like that, stuff which would make me seem real but wouldn't invite any questions on there. For the part of the page where it asks about sexual preferences or whatever I wrote "anything goes". I barely even know what that means because I'm sure that there are some things that I wouldn't ever do. The words were, I don't know, intoxicating, I suppose. Writing it felt better than whatever the fuck it meant to do it, which I didn't even think about anyway.

The man got in touch. He sent an email saying that he was in the same area as me. I had to enter my real postcode. I just wanted to know what things were happening around me. I was really stoned that summer. The guy had just got married and moved into a new house and had a teaching job. I just found it interesting that he was still looking for boys to talk to. He went to the same school as me but had left by the time I started.

He'd send pictures of himself wearing his wife's underwear that just looked stupid. One of them was so funny that I almost showed Luke but then when I realised I couldn't, it kinda reminded me how stupid I was being. He used to ask me stuff that I wanted to do but I didn't know. So he sent me all sorts of things that he used to think about – like which students from his school he wanted to fuck and what he wanted to do to them and all sorts of other things like that. He must have been lonely. At least he was dealing with it, I guess.

Sometimes he'd tell me to meet him and while I was touching my dick I said that I would but as soon as I'd cum, I'd know that it wasn't such a great idea and I'd just end up thinking about Luke or Emma anyway. And his pictures looked so dumb.

I don't know if I could ever meet a stranger like that, I hate how everybody always reminds me of someone.

I want the acid but I'm too stressed to ask. I want to lose everything for a few hours and I want something to share with Luke that might make him remember me but the version of me that doesn't talk about his dead dad all the time. It's too much. I don't know what I'm thinking about.

Alex runs his hand across the cut on his arm. I think about my suit crumpled up at home with the smear of bird's blood on it. I don't think Luke has told Emma that he's come here. He's barely mentioned her, which confuses me, because I'm sure he said earlier that he needed to give her a call. I thought she wanted to come anyway and if Luke had said that he was coming I think that she definitely would have wanted to. I hope he didn't think too much about us hugging at the funeral, but maybe he's still lost and he needs to find himself again bit by bit.

There's something on in the background that nobody is watching because it seems like they all have something in common and are talking about it. Whatever is on TV is talking about old people.

The new guy gives Alex some money. He did it really casual while he was still talking to him. Alex folds up the note and puts it in the pocket of his jeans. Apart from the scar, he has really nice arms, although even the scar is pretty interesting – like it structures something, maybe, like the crack in the CD case. Alex gets up and leaves the room for a couple of minutes and there's a break in the conversation. The new guy looks at me.

"So – are you guys having a late one tonight?"

"Umm ... I don't know." Even when I give answers, it feels like a question.

"Just seeing how it, goes, right?"

"We're just relaxing." That was Luke. It was nice of him. He can probably tell that I'm stoned.

"Oh cool. How do you know Alex?" The new guy said that to me. It seems like it's his mission to get me to actually say something interesting.

"Oh I dunno. Ha. Just from around, you know?."

"Yeah, we've known Alex for a while." Luke completed my sentence.

"Yeah. Alex is cool," I say. "I dunno though – sometimes I worry a little bit too much about him, like, you know – with the drugs I guess." I can hear myself talking but it's just coming out of my mouth like a reflex "And I mean, he's only our age and I know he's already been into some really heavy shit. I think because his parents are rich he's kinda been lucky but I dunno, I do worry, because Alex is really great ... " I feel really hot when I focus on the fact that the new guy is just watching me really confused and Luke is just staring at me like I've gone crazy. I don't know if I even mean the stuff I've just said about Alex. I mean parts of it, but I didn't mean to say anything like that out loud. Alex must have heard me because his place is really small and when he comes in he's looking at me like he just asked a question.

"Are you ok?"

"Yeah – sorry. I'm ..."

"What the fuck?" I guess Alex is really pissed off. Everyone must feel awkward because if I was watching something like this I probably would too.

Alex puts something in the new guy's hand who says thank you and stands up and puts his backpack back on.

"OK. Cool. Thanks man. Nice meeting you two." When he says that he looks at me for a little longer than he does at Luke. "If you're having a late night, then have a good time." He leaves and Alex sits down and looks at me. He shakes his head and looks at the TV.

No-one says anything for at least two minutes, both of which feel like five and then Alex turns back to me.

"I mean – what did you say stuff like that for?" I feel so stupid and embarrassed.

"I don't know. I think ... I don't know. I think that I was ..." I trail off and try to work it out but it's hard to with Alex looking at me like he wants to hit me and Luke sitting there like he's not sure what to do.

"It's just been a fucked up day." Luke said that, and I guess Alex has to back down because Luke managed to phrase stuff in such a calm way that it's almost insane. "The funeral was fucked up. The last few ... I don't know – everything has been fucked up, you know?"

Alex is looking at Luke. He already seems less angry, more frail.

"And Alex, the thing is — we have worried about you sometimes, man. I mean we haven't heard from you in a long time and we gave up trying to get in touch because you never answered the phone and one time me and Emma came round and we thought you were in but someone else answered the door and said that you weren't. You just get a general feeling when someone isn't ok."

I want to hold onto Luke and never let him go. It's like I'm not in the room for the next minute or so that he's talking to Alex. I don't understand how he just works out how to solve problems and just slot them back into place. I suppose they're sorting things out as I think this.

Alex stands up and walks over to me and crouches down and gives me a small hug that throws me off guard but still feels welcome. He's saying to forget about things and that everyone was just a little strained for their own different reasons. Luke looks stressed but like he knows it's ok now. I feel bad that he's the one with the dead dad and he's having to hold things together for other people, though maybe the one thing is the extension of the other for him.

Alex is still kneeling next to me. He clinks his drink of wine against mine. That means stuff is fine. That's meant to be like the last bit of sellotape on our fracture. I still feel like I'm just waking up from something nasty though. I can't relax.

It's feels like so long since I last did drugs with Luke. The last time we did it, it was also Alex who got them for us. We took ecstasy. That was after Luke had driven us to these woods a couple of hours from where we lived. It was around the time that he was first getting together with Emma. I remember he kept sending her messages while he was driving, slowing down and tapping on his phone, speeding up again and then slowing down and tapping on his phone again. When we got to the place we were going there was no signal so he turned his phone off. We took the pills and listened to music and things felt amazing.

About twenty minutes later when everything is calmer and Alex seems like he's forgotten that he was angry he pulls a tiny plastic bag out of his pocket. It's the acid. He flicks the bag over to Luke. Luke catches it and holds it up in front of him. He's looks like something's funny.

"Who's behind this stuff? Haha. A fucking *bicycle*?" Luke passes me the baggy. I hold it in my palm and look at the acid. It's a piece of blotter paper with a picture of a cartoon man sitting on a cartoon bike.

"I know, heh." Alex says. "The last stuff I had had a pirate on it. That skull and cross bones seemed like a threat." Alex and Luke both laugh at that but I'm still looking at the man on the bike. He looks like he's wobbling, really insanely. The wheels are twisted in different directions.

"Have you tried any of this?"

"No. But the guy that sold it me said that it's pretty strong. So I think it should be pretty good." Alex makes a joke about something to do with consciousness that I don't get and I don't think he does either. I laugh though, just to show that I'm not worrying about him like I said I was before. I don't even think that I am. Sometimes I think that I just talk because it feels like silence might be working against me, or giving me too much time for something else destructive.

"So ..." I pass the acid to Alex who tears down the thin perforated lines and separates the man on the bike into lots of little bits. He puts one in his mouth and hands the bag to me. I put one on my tongue and pass the bag to Luke. For a second I have this horrible feeling that Luke has decided not to take any of the acid and will get up and go home. His face looks worn-out for a moment, completely sapped, but he does this little smirk or snort to himself like that doesn't mean anything and pops a tab in his mouth which then becomes a big grin.

I just noticed something about Alex. It's his hands. They're unclean. Yellowed at the tips. His nails are long and there's dirt underneath them. He's fiddling with a coin. He spins it round on this little coffee table that's covered in bits of tobacco and torn up bits of paper and crumbs. The coin doesn't seem to spin for too long. Sometimes he fumbles it and it won't spin at all.

Alex's decline has got so much to do with suburbia. I know that people have to look at themselves. He chose certain things and got lost in them. Maybe other things were in the way. But suburbia pretends that everything has limits, like the lots of land it's made up of. People get tricked. My parents are still fooled. Maybe Alex still thinks that everything is ok.

I don't need to squint that hard to see what Alex was like as a child. It's almost simple, which throws me. He looks more tired than old. Still fidgeting around. He looks cuddly and feral.

"So what have you been doing?" Luke might have been thinking the same thing as me. Only he's the one that said it.

"When?"

"Ever."

"Ha. Umm. Not much. Just the usual, really. Nothing as bad as what people probably thought."

"Have you still been seeing people much?"

"Not for a while. I've not been avoiding anyone though."

"Right."

"I saw Mark quite a lot. Well, sometimes we'd hang out."

I don't think I know who Mark is, but I guess Luke must do.

"Oh, cool. I've not seen him for a while." They both talk about this person I don't know. I stare around the room a little bit. There's a bookshelf that looks like stuff would fall off if you tried to remove even one of the books. There are more CDs on there than books. The books that there are, are all either really bashed up and tatty or brand new. There's no in-between. I think one of the books might be Luke's. It's about a band that he likes. I try to think of a question so that he doesn't zone out. The fact that I think that makes me realise that I'm not in a good mood, or highlights it more than it already was.

"So was your dad buried or cremated?"

"Cremated."

"How come?"

"I don't know. He wanted to be."

"Oh, did he know he was dying?"

"No. It's just one of those things he would say. I want to be cremated. He let us know for future reference."

I always get nervous after I've taken drugs. Like I'm walking on a ground that I know is meant to be uneven, I start stepping slowly, thinking I'll fall. You can get too careful if you don't keep an eye on yourself. It doesn't last long though.

I stand up and walk to Alex's bathroom. There are little drops of piss on the basin. I lock the door. I look at the mirror and try and smile to myself, pretending it's a moment from a film. I'm not sure why I wanted to pretend. I do it sometimes, like I'm checking that

I can trust myself now that I've taken the acid. Making sure I know where I am and who I am, which is a sober thing. I hate the fact that I probably don't seem myself to anyone. I decide that when I leave the bathroom I'll try and make myself seem more awake to them. I piss.

On the way back through the house I notice the blue light of a computer screen in Alex's bedroom. I want to go in and see what Craig has replied, because by now he'll have had the time to think about the things that I said to him and he'll have sent something back. It's crazy.

Someone calls my name so I wonder back into the room.

Luke has put on a CD. He's kneeling next to the stereo looking so amazing and smiling, mouthing some words to himself. They must be important. The music is some punk band. I like them more than most of the other stuff that I used to listen to, because it never sounds like they're telling people what to do. They sound just as lost as they should be. Alex sits in his chair and nods like he's still feeling his way into it. He spins the coin on the table again but again it falls off.

Luke is tapping the tops of his legs like they're drums.

"This bit is incredible." The guitars start doing something really loud. It is pretty amazing. And the singer sounds like he's trying not to cry but — maybe because I can see Luke likes it so much — he doesn't sound like he's doing an impression. It feels nice to hear. He's shouting about how nothing makes sense. Luke looks puzzled by how much something in the music is affecting him. He realises that he must look pretty stupid and laughs. I feel good.

"I'm glad I came out tonight," Luke says. "I needed this." He's not talking about the music. It feels like I'm helping with whatever it is that I'm meant to be helping with and I have to fight the urge to just go and grab Luke and hug him. I smile. I'm drunk.

"Me too. I've missed you." I sound clumsy but Luke knows what I mean because his smiles alters to a different one that says that he does. It's definitely more freighted.

The acid must be strong, because I can feel the effects quickly. The first time I notice anything is when I'm looking at Luke and I just feel different somehow. His face is really lit up. He's feeling it too. I say something to Alex about feeling it and he nods his head and grins and then nods again like I said something else.

"Can you feel that?"

"Yeah – like – yeah. Ha."

"God. Shit. Haha."

"So is this stuff going to be strong?"

"What?"

"Strong? Haha."

"Strong."

"He said is this stuff going to be strong?"

"Haha. Yeah. It's meant to be pretty strong, yeah."

"Yeah. I can tell this stuff is gonna be pretty strong. Strong. Heh."

I sit back in the chair for a second to ground myself. I can tell that everyone feels excited which is cool and puts my mood in a totally different place. I did some test on the internet once that said I was an enthusiast, and that I really feed off other people when they're happy or into something or having a good time. It works the other way but that's not happening now. An enthusiast could also be understood as a parasite.

My hand feels shaky probably because I'm nervous. I have another sip of the sour wine. It tastes sharp and I wince but it feels like a celebration. Luke is sitting and looking up slightly at the wall next to him like he's waiting for something or as if he hadn't seen it before. Alex reaches over and picks up the remote control and starts flicking channels. In a strange parody of the savants' faces, the sound is cheerful but muted.

10

Cherry red shoes. A car park. A certain type of light.

11

It's faster and stronger than I thought. Last time it took longer to get this far. The music stopped. I don't know when. The television is loud. Alex put on God TV because he thought it would be funny to watch American Christians shouting about sin. It isn't. *Flick.*

The man looks like a pig. He looks like he's a puppet, made by those animatronics studios that make stuff for films, monsters and demons, or whatever. His skin looks rubbery and sweaty. Someone must have splashed some drink on their puppet. It's funny. He's ugly. I'm trying to work out where his eyes are. His forehead overhangs and his face is all pushed up. Part of me feels bad for laughing; the guy is just trying to read the weather.

This is happening fast.

Luke's on his hands and his knees like he's praying. He's rubbing his hands round on the carpet over and over again, moving his palms along the ground like he's feeling out shapes of trying to find inconsistencies in the ones he's discovered. His eyes are moving around like crazy. He looks so dumb and funny and goofy that I get off my chair and try to do the same thing.

Moving from the chair was stranger than I expected. Everything jolted. It's as if we're all held up by liquid that can't be moved. I can see the carpet now and it must be what he sees. Its red with some boring design that is coming to life like flowers, just quivering a bit but in this really incredible way like it's a pool or a painting, something impressionist in either light.

Dizzy without stopping.

Things feel like they're circling to towards the TV in patterns or puddles. When I look up its as though a wind had distracted me. I stretch my mouth open and grind my bottom jaw a couple of times, which I think releases endorphins but I have might have remembered that wrong, but still, for a second, it's like I've taken ecstasy anyway and I think that's what I might have been thinking grinding my jaw would do or hoping that it might be like.

I pick up my wine and drink a bit more even though it strikes me as pointless. When I swallow, something feels wrong, or unexpected. At first I think that it feels like I swallowed a hair that must have been in my glass. Something really thin down my throat. I gulp a couple of times to get rid of whatever it is but whatever it is just brushes or scrapes without pain against my tonsils. It makes me think of tinsel from the Christmas trees but only because nothing else comes to mind.

The world is rotational. Dizzy without stopping.

When I blink it's like strobe lights.

I turn to Luke and he just pulls this face that looks like he's helpless but he wants to – I was going to say something else but I think it scared me – but he definitely looks like he wants to laugh real hard. It's funny and I'm trying to think more about balance.

If we were in a film then there would be a close up of Luke's face and then an extreme close-up because that's what my world is for however many seconds it is that I've been staring at him for. He's fucking perfect and it hurts so much sometimes but right now it makes sense in a really clear way that I'm trying to keep grasp of.

"Hahahahahahaha." Alex pauses for breath "Shiiiit. Haha. This is fucked."

Alex is standing up but I don't remember seeing him move. He looks dizzy but that could be because my eyes are moving too fast with him in them. When I think about him and Emma together it feels like the walls are closing in – that's not anything to do with the acid, it's just I feel claustrophobic like it takes everything I have? to think about them and sometimes it feels like it stops me from breathing. They've flickered in and out from time to time when I've been masturbating so I know that it must turn me on to imagine them together. But I think I try and pretend that it doesn't because I'm jealous of how much better my disappearance makes people appear together. And I guess it hurts to be truthful with myself about that, because the jealousy doesn't want to share certain things with any other part of my brain. I'll pretend that I can hate them both for it which makes things worse because I know that I don't and I can't. It also makes me feel like a hypocrite but I try to keep that well hidden from myself. I feel bad because I know I'm being false when I try to pretend that my lies are more truthful than their lies. I'm thinking about lies to do with Alex and Emma and therefore Luke.

"Luke – are you ok? Haha."

"Heh. Yeah, I think so – haha."

The bass of the music that's replaced the TV again sounds like an elastic band. It tickles. That's the coolest thing about acid, the way that music gets fucked around. I keep having to move my head, turn it, stretch. The music feels like it's dismantling. It's all just whirring and cogs – I think it's just some band – not even any of the noise stuff that Luke sometimes plays, that stuff might make sense at this moment. It'd be levelled out by all of this interference the drug conducts through the world.

The sensation when I swallow is still happening every time. Maybe my throat has tightened. That happened when I took mushrooms one time. It already feels like this has been happening for a long time, like the drug has aged me. It already feels like this has been happening for a long time.

Alex walks out of the room. Luke is staying put so I do to. In a way anything could be happening now that Alex is out of sight. I just want to stay with Luke. I want to share this with him. I want to hold his face in mine. I put my tingling hands out and put them on his shoulders. He flinches which feels like I've been tickled and he looks at me. He puts his arms round me and hugs me so tightly that everything feels how I wish it always did. I wonder if I'd be able to fuck, feeling like this. I've pretty much forgotten about my sex, so it's like I just woke up from something. I'm more sensitive to Luke's hands now. I can feel them grabbing at my back firmly. It feels so good. I do the same to his. Like I'm pushing them into him and massaging whatever is under the flesh; bones and blood then. It's intense. I just realised that I don't feel afraid of anything.

One of us says the word "fuck". Luke pulls himself away and starts looking at his hands. I don't know if he's seeing the same thing as me but it's almost double, like there are slight trails every time that he moves his fingers. He wiggles them a few times.

"See?"

"Yeah." He must be seeing the same as me. It doesn't matter if he isn't.

This is happening fast.

I hear a sound. The toilet flushing. Water. Pipes. Water going through pipes. Alex stands in the doorway and says something about the bathroom. I don't want to see it.

"Haha. Really?" Luke stands up and walks towards the bathroom. I don't want him to go, but I sit still and just feel a rush of this feeling that undoubtedly could pick me up if it wanted to. Alex moves out of Luke's way, kinda leans against the doorframe like he's flirting but I think that's just my imagination because Luke walks into the bathroom and laughs at something, maybe the same as what Alex had spoken about, and no further chemistry follows.

"Sorry – I gotta piss ... heh." Luke closed the door and I hear the bolt lock. Alex walks towards me and stands still again. He keeps doing that.

"This is strong? Has it started really fast? Right? This is happening really fast?"

"Yeah." Alex answers as if I just asked him something he'd never thought about before but I think he must have and he might be again now.

"Man, haha. This is so fucking ..."

"Yeah ..."

"I know ..."

"Yeah ..."

" ..."

"…"

"…………

…………"

That was weird.

"………………………………………………………………………"

"………………………………………………………………………"

"…………………………

………………………………"

"…………

……………………"

"Fuck."

"Yeah I know. Haha."

"So have you had this stuff before?"

"Acid?"

The word sounds so dumb – it doesn't capture any of this, but I still say, "Yeah – acid." Maybe it captures the sense of corrosion but not the idea.

"Ummm, yeah."

"No – I mean … I don't mean acid. I mean – acid? Haha. No."

"………………

………………"

"Yeah it is weird."

"Yeah I know."

"I mean – this type of acid. This stuff that we've had now. That's happening. That acid."

"Oh … no. Not this acid."

"Yeah. That's what I meant."

"Yeah, cool. But no. I've not."

We both laugh.

Luke's still in the bathroom but I feel distracted by other stuff. I mean, as well as that. For a second this certain and tiny bit of light hits Alex's face at a precise angle and just makes his face look like a skull, like his skin is just tracing paper that's hardly there at all, yet all kinds of things have been etched all over it.

"What can you see?" When he speaks it stops.

"Haha. I don't even know. The carpet is ..."

"Yeah I had that before. Like it's moving or ..."

"Yeah."

I usually find it so hard to believe anything that I think.

But.

At the moment I feel like I can trust myself and everything around me because things have clicked into place and I suppose it feels for the first time like nothing is my fault.

Luke is still in the bathroom. Alex says something about going to look at stuff and gets up. I don't want to be left on my own so I stand up and walk with him through to the bedroom. There are a load of posters on the wall, some that I remember and some that could have been here the last time I came over but that I might have forgotten about. They could also be new. It's messy – worse than the front room where we'd been sitting. Alex is probably used to it. He doesn't mention the mess. He puts his arm out and runs his fingers against one of the walls. I do the same to the wall on the opposite side of the room. It feels wet. I look at my fingers. They don't look damp. I put them back on the wall and they feel cold again. I look at them again and think of the coin that fell on the table earlier, which tickles. I think about the bird but that freaks me out so much that I block? against the thought as hard as I can till it's ... gone? My fingers aren't wet. This time I push harder on the wall. There are shadows of fingers now. They leave smudges that aren't actually on the wall – they hover just over it. It's awesome.

Alex kneels down next to the bed. His legs are on the floor and his torso flopped on the mattress. He stretches his arms out and for two seconds it looks like he's pretending to swim but then hops his top half up so he's leaning on his elbows.

"It's fucked up about Luke's dad."

"Yeah." I don't know why he's bringing up that stuff.

"So you went to the funeral?"

"Yeah." It feels fucked up like Alex must be some kinda of

masochist to want to even think about the funeral at this moment? in time.

"That was fucking today, man? That's fucked up, right?" He grins but I can't tell if that's the acid or if he actually wants to smile while he talks about the funeral.

"Yeah."

"Fuck man."

"Yeah I know. It was ..." I feel afraid of whatever words I didn't say even though I didn't know what they were going to be. I stopped myself anyway.

"How was Luke?"

"I dunno."

"I know, I know," I don't know if he was listening to what I said. He just nods his head and repeats himself. "But how is he? How has he been coping with everything? I mean – you know – just death in general or whatever?"

"He's in the bathroom." When I said that, it sounded like a question.

"I know man! You just said that! You keep repeating the same things!"

"Do I?" I don't even know anymore. I could believe it. I don't remember it though.

"Yes!" He almost scowls which really fucks me up.

"Sorry – I'm all over the place."

"No man it's cool. I was just wondering how Luke was doing that was all."

"Yeah."

"I wasn't – I mean – I can tell you don't want to talk about it so I'll drop it." It feels like an argument just appeared from nowhere and died out again but is still hanging around. It's stopped. But I can still feel it.

I kneel down next to Alex and I put my hand on his. A peace offering? His hand feels warm, like his skin is the softest thing I've ever touched. I rub mine against his. He stretches his fingers out and I rub mine all over them. I hold his index finger and rub my hand up and down it a few times. It feels amazing and I guess it does for Alex too, if the look on his face is anything to go by which I guess it is. His eyes are closed and his mouth is just a little bit open. His breathing is louder and a little like rain outside a window. Pittering. Pittering. Pit-ter-ing. Pit. Ter. Ing. In and out.

The visuals are really kicking in. There's a poster on the wall. It's some cartoon that Alex likes. It was brightly coloured already but now it's glowing. The colours are all standing out of the poster like blocks. Some colours are further out than others. It's like a 3D bar chart. The pink is furthest out, then a really bright green. Red is closest to the wall. One of the cartoon characters stands above a stream. I think it's a cat. The stream is bluer than anything and fluorescent. It's flowing, but like a zigzag and not like water.

The tips of my fingers rub across the tips of Alex's fingers. His nails feel like a clue to something I didn't know was unsolved. I go over them and over again a few times. We're both trembling.

T/r/e/m/b/l/i/n/g/

Alex makes this noise like a grunt that makes me think he's answering a question that I'm not sure if I asked one or not. It happened earlier I think. But now it's now. This is all something to do with repetition.

The way that Alex is letting me touch his fingers is making me think that maybe we could fuck each other. Now that I've announced that out loud in my brain stuff seems a lot more powerful. That's why I've been keeping other names at the back of my brain because I know that it's wrong to admit to things if you really don't want to think about them. So I'm holding his hand now and rubbing my thumb around in his palm. I let go and stretch out my hand so my fingers are pointing out life a leaf that's fallen from tree and got frozen in mid-air. He pulls his nails across my hand and I must make some kind of gasp because Alex laughs a little bit. When I look at him we both must look so like we understand the confusion really well that it shocks us because he falls back a little bit and sits on the floor staring at me. He takes his hand away but I still stare at him the same.

"Are you ok?" That was me.

"Yeah."

Alex looks like he's looking at something that's really funny but maybe more strange than funny. He's squinting. I want to know what he's seeing and I want to know if I'm looking at it as well. I squint one of my eyes to ask a question and his eyebrows both raise and he does this grin that for about two seconds is actually terrifying but then it switches to hilarious and we both start laughing. I put my hand on his leg almost without thinking about it.

"You want me to shut the door?" The way he said it sounded like he was questioning something that I just suggested but for about the millionth time I didn't say anything or am confused as to whether I did or not. Alex pushes the door shut and the sound it makes when it finally slams makes me shudder. Every sound is like music because it's all in little keys turned around my brain.

"What are you saying ... like ... you ... ?" I think it was a question but I still think I'm just looking at Alex. I can't remember much about my own body right now so it's hard to tell.

Being a ghost must be easy.

"What do you mean no one would know?" I don't know if Alex saying that means that we're going to fuck because it sounds like he's just repeating stuff that I said and it's getting harder and harder to understand because he obviously thinks that I'm suggesting these things and I can't tell if I've said anything but I'm looking at him and I've still got my hand on his leg and I think I'm rubbing it but that could just be what touch feels like right now which could be something completely different. I realise how fragile his leg feels like I could probably break it if I wanted to, or just pull it apart like it's a cushion filled with cotton and feathers. If I'd wanted to and if I wasn't worried about touching the blood and feeling the maggots squirming around and falling up my sleeves I could have put my hands inside the dead bird and pulled it apart to get a better idea of the small assembly inside.

Maybe it just died and fell in flight and there's no fucking mystery at all. Maybe dead birds just fall in flight.

When people are horny anything seems potential.

"You're saying no one would have to know?"

"No one would have to know?" I repeated it that time, I don't know if I'm mimicking Alex or myself.

I hear the sound of the door shutting again and get the same shudder even though they're both things that have already happened and didn't just happen again.

Pittering.

Pattering.

There are explosions of something that tickles but in a visual way I can't see, in my stomach. Alex is much closer than he was whenever I last thought about that stuff. His eyes are huge, especially the centres. I forget whether there was music playing before because I can't tell if there is now or not. I'm so close to kissing Alex and I can feel my nails scratching and clutching against the top of his leg which is crossed over the other one which just makes me think of a heap of bones. Alex blinks.

B/l/i/n/k/s

Open.

And.

Closed.

Open.

And.

Closer.

When you're on acid. No. When I am. When I am on acid

everything feels like words. But it feels like every single word has got apostrophes in the wrong places. There was something I read. It was on the internet? Maybe it was in school. Maybe someone showed me. If you keep the first and the last letters of a word in the same place, but you mix up the letters in the middle, people will still be able to recognize the word. I don't know if acid is like that. It's both. As in it is and it isn't like that. Which *does* make acid like that mixed up word. I can tell what all these words are but I can't at the same time.

Something happens. Either I kissed Alex or he's on the other side of the room. Oth'r s'de 'f th' r"m.

Whether a band is punk or not depends on how you think about music, not if you do.

The bar chart of a poster is still hovering about, divided into about 6 different continents of colour.

Someone just said something that made so little sense that I got it completely. Alex. He's here, after all. Weird how all this looks. I shoot my eyes around the room a lot. When I was younger I used to draw a lot of pictures.

My shoulders tense up. Fuck. Because I don't quite remember something.

I relax again when I hear that the music has changed. It's nothing now. Maybe I don't recognize it.

There's still this really horny feeling that feels ... sincere? Maybe just earnest. Everyone has been trained to miss something that they never actually had but they've been told so many times that they're not complete without it that they'll never ever be able to feel as special as they should and they are and probably could really be able to so I put my head against Alex. I think we're supposed to kiss, or maybe we did, but now my head is on his shoulder. It's easier.

"Where's Emma?"

"..."

"How's Emma?"

".."

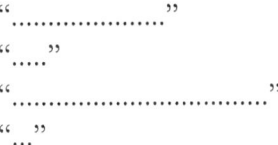

"where'semmahow'semma?"

That hurts and everything feels like the ... the inside of ... some shape? that I can't quite feel out. Maybe it's dark inside every shape but people spend too much time looking at how many sides there are, so they can work out what shape they're looking at.

I think I make Alex feel something that is closer to Emma for him. Cold air fizzing on the inside of my skull. I always try not to think too much about bones. Skulls just freak me out. We're all interiors. Hard to feel the direction of the breeze because it's all at once.

Everything is at once.

Everything is so close that I can barely make it out.

Everything just works.

Everything just is.

Everything is.

Everything is cold.

Everything is infused.

Everything is constant.

Everything is electricity.

Everything is stretched till it loses shape.

Everything is shapes.

Everything has sides.

Everything is sides.

Everything is friction.

Everything is everything else.

Everything is burning.

Everything is beautiful.

Everything is distressing.

Everything is shadows.

Everything is internet.

119

Everything is waiting.

Everything is forever.

Everything is sincere.

Everything is not watching the things it's creating.

He picks something up. He puts it down. He looks at it. I look at it. I think I'm learning something. He might be too. I don't pick it up because I can't tell if he's going to again. He doesn't but thinks about it. I think about it too. He puts a hand back on it. I think I feel it. We're learning the same thing. Cubed? No – but I can feel it. We're both so nervous, wrapping our eyes round it like we want them or it to stretch out somehow.

T/r/e/m/b/le

If I look somewhere else it looks like the light in the room has been put through a paper shredder and is sprinkled down in its new shape of strips; or like a TV fucking up in bad weather. Tinsel swallows still like tinsel. Tinsel isn't the right word. It hasn't become the right word yet. I think it might have been the right word. It just hasn't become the right word yet.

"Yeah – she's fine. Emma."

"She didn't want to ..." Alex trails off. Laughter/his.

I'm really scared.

"Didn't want to?" I'm waiting for him to answer I think.

Alex laughs some more.

"To come!"

I know what Alex means, but I'm stuck with the word cum. I think of Emma in this blur that almost feels like I'm trying to stop myself from thinking of her. I think of her cumming. I think of her whole body tensing up over Alex. I think of his face looking hot, red, tired then I try the same image with his face cocky, confident, sure, Emma's legs crossing round his. Crunching themselves together really slowly. Her hips grinding at his like she was trying to work his cock down to nothing. Something about the curve of Emma's back – damp, glazed. I don't even know if they actually ever fucked. It doesn't matter, I guess, because most things seem to be separated from love and I know that I don't love Alex, although I guess I probably would if I found out that he loved me. I feel like Alex probably knows Emma more than I ever could.

Huh? He wants to phone Emma?

"You wanna/call/her?"

"Yeah/ok"

"What?"

"Do I wanna/call her?"

"Yeah."

"Yeah."

Watching TV again. Feral game show savant. More/tastes/metallic. Gone. Strong winds holding things up/more metal/tinsel. Taste but no object. Alex has got these really great arms, and when he wears red, it makes them look even better. Things, I guess, are this way just because they are.

I think about asking Alex whether he and Emma slept with each other. I think about what would happen if I asked it and he answered me. I think about what his answers would make me feel like. Things feel almost in order just for a few seconds. Seconds feel longer than seconds so that's fine. Seconds are just ... There's this part of me that just feels like a snow globe. I'm sort of calm and level, but the smallest thing makes everything shake and it rains all this confused but beautiful stuff. I guess being confused must be beautiful. It's just complicated trying to see things properly when you're basically a glass ball.

Alex stands and flops back onto the bed so his legs are hanging off the edge. Part of me feels like I just told him how madly in love with Emma I am, even though at the moment it feels clear to me that I'm not. I think I just want to be loved more than anything. But then everything about me tells me that's not what I want.

"We should go outside."

It feels like I'm being guided down the street with Alex. He's holding my arm with his. We're like bonds of a chain? Everything is so cold. The street's swirling. I'm lost in this place completely. I'm sure we walk past an arguing couple, just round the corner from where Alex lives.

I open my eyes. I didn't realise that they were closed.

I'm still on the floor in Alex's bedroom. I think he got up and walked out the room. Either that or he's behind me. My eyes feel like they're closing again and the colours on the wall are all nothing but growing around me.

We're back in the street and I'm worried that someone is going to talk to us or one of us will fall over and need someone to pick us back up again. I think I do fall over. Sludgy mess from the top of a drain. Tiny pieces of gravel imprinted on my palm. It's probably raining because it wasn't earlier.

A hand that it turns out is mine touches the poster that's been flashing and vibrating so much just outside my eyesight. It feels smooth and cold. The colours move somewhere else while I'm trying to touch them. It feels flat. I turn my hand round and stroke the surface with the back of my hand. It makes the poster feel smoother. I try the wall around the poster. When I was younger I would never have imagined that I'd be in this situation. That doesn't mean that I think the situation I'm in is important. I'm just saying. I wouldn't have imagined this. There isn't the scope you suppose to things.

Alex is shouting. Me too. I think my voice is doing the work for both of us. I feel like I can't speak. I'm trying to scream but nothing is coming out. Someone has turned the volume down or whatever is in my throat has stopped it working. I think it might be because we're outside and the cold and the rain have frozen whatever is stuck in my throat. Yes. It's too cold to work properly, my throat, out here.

I'm definitely inside.

I think the couple that are arguing have turned and stared at us. One of the pair is on the street on the opposite side to us. The other is leaning out of a window shouting down at the other person. I think they're arguing about love. If she fell I don't think it would hurt. I worry that if we're staring at them then we're staring for too long. They're already angry enough. We walk down to a corner of a street where about three others begin – forward, left, and right.

TREM/BLE
TRE/MBLE
T R E M B L E
TREMB/LE

Alex says something about walking to somebody's house. It must be someone we know but I still can't believe that we're out here so I'm having enough trouble trying to work that stuff out.

There's a bang that sounds like a door closing. It's the first time there's been no music. I thought it had happened before, but now it has in a way that seems more first than prior. Someone has closed a door and I feel more alone than I did before. I'm definitely alone. But it's ok because I'm feeling all this shit that seems to make more sense without other people. If someone else was here it would just make it feel like I have to show evidence of what I'm going through, to them and to myself.

I get on my knees and put my face on the bed. My body follows. I get this rush and want it to last. My heart feels electronic, like the beat of some terrible trance music. It's the repetition that gets me though. It starts sounding like something else when it's lined up next to a million identical things. I think I hear Alex fiddling around with something elaborate in the next room.

I think I fall over again. The water from the street soaks into my jeans, so that they feel heavy. It's like things keep trying to pull me back onto the floor. Alex stumbles at one point and uses my arm to keep him up and falls into a lamppost, laughing, mainly to himself. The two people arguing are further down the street now. We moved and they stayed still.

Every thought feels like it's coming from a hollowed out place or a metal tube that echoes like a ghost clinking around inside a glass of water.

I want to be surrounded by old photos of people that I've never met. I don't want the people I care for to have pasts. I don't want people I'm in love with to have cried before I knew them – I don't want the people I love to have ever needed me when I wasn't there, to have ever have needed me. Loving isn't selfish, I don't think, unless being selfish is pure or something. It's this drill you drive through yourself.

"I had this thing –"

"Yeah?"

"Yeah. Your face." Your face///"

"You had my face? You're so ruined."

L/a/u/g/h/s

"No."

"What are you talking about?"/those words a hundred times at once.

"My face?"

"Yeah."

"Start again."

"Yeah."

"OK."

"I had this thing about your face."

"Haha – " splinters off somewhere.

"I kept thinking you and Luke had changed faces."

Stops. Think about whether I said it or not. Feel shivers. They're from the cold. They're nothing to do with what I can't remember I said.

"Haha – say again, sorry. I'm fucked." Makes me remember.

"Oh yeah,"

"Haha."

"I thought that Luke was really starting to look like you?"

"Luke's in the bathroom?"

"God – heh," I start wondering about how long it's been since I saw Luke.

"You mean tonight?" Preoccupied now.

"He's in the bathroom tonight, yeah."

"I mean our faces."

"Oh, yeah. No. Not tonight. I meant before. I hadn't seen you in a while ..."

" ..."

"And your faces. I thought you'd swapped. Which I know is stupid. I've seen both of you tonight and I know I was just being stupid."

"You're fucked."

"Yeah."

"No. I mean tonight."

"I haven't seen you for a while."

"I know. Man."

"I want to see Luke."

I stand up which means the room does too. I stand up again and this time it works better. Anything outside of what I can see needs to stop. Alex has disappeared, he's probably crawling somewhere. I put my hand on the wall of the corridor that links the rooms in the flat, and reach out my other hand to even things out. The bathroom door is unlocked so I go in. Luke's kneeling on the floor wobbling. He's unsteady, which added to my vision right now makes him look a little bit like a flame or how hot air makes things look blurry like waves.

For a few seconds Luke doesn't realise I'm there but then he catches me in a mirror that's leant up against a dirty radiator. It makes him jump which does the same to me. He turns round and I kneel down with him. He's been crying. I wonder if he knows I can't help him.

"I heard the door before – did you go somewhere?"

"I think Alex took me outside ... but I don't know."

It can't matter much because Luke doesn't say anything. His eyes have this look that says things that I probably won't ever be able to explain to him. Maybe eyes are the same as words. Luke looks around the room. He shivers. It makes me feel cold. I want to know what the right thing to do is. Luke seems lost in something that I must be seeing differently. I think about the email I sent to Craig and worry about whether he read it. I think about where the computer is in all of this.

My hand feels warm. Luke's holding it. One of our hands is clammy. I ask how he's feeling because I feel like I need to say something and then feel like it was the most pointless question I could have asked. Luke looks down and doesn't say anything. I hope it's because he forgotten the question.

"I'm cold." Luke stands up, taking me with him. We both stretch our arms. Luke's arms are one of his best physical features. I've always liked watching people stretch. One of the first times I realised that I might have been ... whatever the fuck I am ... was when I saw some boy in P.E. doing a handstand against the wall. The school P.E. kit was red shorts and white t-shirt. His feet kicked against the wall and his t-shirt hung upside down so anyone in the class who was looking would have seen his body. It was all stretched out – his stomach and his chest. I think one of the girls made a joke about him looking boney or something ... but I couldn't stop thinking about him for ... ever? So now I like how Luke looks when his arms are stretched.

Memories/swallowing is ... still crazy/really fast slow motion/.

We move into the front room. I think about this being the room where things started. I'm glad the TV isn't on. Is there music? No. Luke rattles round in a pile of CDs that must have fallen over. They're on the floor. I sit and watch him and hope that he'll come back to me when he's done.

The CD cases clicking together sound like someone tapping on bone. Mine? Luke's?

Luke chooses some music. The cover is a black and white photo of a rundown looking building in a city. It looks like it's half way through falling down or being demolished. It's kinda blank. It looks cheaply made too, or just like people might have paid a lot of money for the CD to look like it was cheaply done. Art is weird.

When the music starts my spine fizzes. S/t/r/e/t/c/h some

more. Computer music. Some songs made on a laptop, but from the way Luke is squinting, like he's trying to see the notes coming out of the speakers, I can tell it must be more than just mechanical.

Things would be so perfect if no one ever said anything ever again. The way things are at this precise second in time, this exact moment ‒t-h-i-s-s-s-e-x-a-c-c-cccccccccccccccccc-t ‒ momennnnn/t ‒ I wish I could keep things like this forever. It's gone.

So the music feels like rain made out of plastic. Stuff falling, but not real ‒ or real ‒ but designed ‒ made to feel like something it's not, thus real.

I want to show Luke Craig's photographs. I want to try and explain how I feel so lost and I really feel like I'm going insane because I'm so lonely and I'm so afraid at how I feel so stupid that I don't understand anything about myself or anyone else or anything else I or they feel. I want to be able to tell him why there has to be a cartoon on my profile and not a real picture of myself. I want to ask Luke if he noticed the dead bird and what he thought about it and whether or not he's thought about it as much as I have. I want to ask Luke if he got the same email as me, and whether or not he thought it was funny or if he wished the ending hadn't been a joke because what came before seemed so ... the right words haven't ... s/t/r/e/t/c/h/e/d/?

Words are doing bad impressions.

12

I changed the entry on Wikipedia about birds so that there's a section on there now that just reads: Death; and underneath: *a dead bird falls in flight.* It's half a haiku. As un-intriguing as it may sound to you, it feels really perfect and sad and special to me. It doesn't matter if you hate it. Someone will change it back again.

13

Thinking about if this feeling in my throat was a colour and if it was it would be glitter/purple/green. My glittery hand print on one of Emma's breasts. Print moves down to her stomach. The colour's changed by this room because that's where I imagine her. Dirty carpet, sweat. I have this feeling that there's no way of getting away from things even if, especially if they're things that I've made happen myself. Things don't do anything except fall apart, even when they come together. I'm only just starting to notice that emotions do what people say they do, which means that I think I must have misunderstood something and ... someone says something and I can't tell whether it's a joke or not, so I don't laugh just in case it isn't and I try to do this smile that says if it is a joke then I get it and if it isn't a joke then I understand that it isn't. I keep noticing that I'm hard but it seems more engulfing than ... Emma's down on all fours and Luke and Alex are both fucking her. I think I love anyone who shows me anything approaching the same thing I'm feeling because I'm so lost and I'm desperate for anyone to help me, even though I don't know where I'm trying to get back to, or what good their help would do. There are hints everywhere. I think Emma likes me because I make her feel complicated, I mean, like know it. She's complicated enough, already, but she doesn't see that – she loves Alex and Luke because she wants to fuck them and loves me because I want to fuck her. I think that's it. Although she probably doesn't love Alex. She likes the fact that he likes her and he's her type or something. I'm not her type. Her type is more ... Hmm. Maybe all of this has been about me... Yet everything feels mechanical. I hate the idea of Emma ever thinking about the dead actor. I get the feeling that I could do a better job of being that unreal. It's the part of him that's so reachable that hurts the most. I want to be near a computer. I told Craig stuff that I didn't really mean. Or I tried to sound different to what I mean. I wanted to sound like someone else. Maybe that means that I sounded exactly how I do. I think about if they found Emma's body when they found the actor's she could be underneath him. That bit almost made me laugh because it's so stupid like the sort of thing someone would make up if they were only thinking about people dying as a way of ... Emma's tits are so – sincere? I think about that one time that I think we kissed, well I know we did but I don't know if she ever thinks about it or even remembers it and if she doesn't I worry that it might mean it doesn't exist like when people talk about trees falling down or when I think about the white cubes and how I wish I could sleep inside one of them and how the art probably meant the wrong thing to me and I wish I could smell Emma really closely like my head in between her legs with her sitting down and I picture myself as Craig which makes me remember how hard I feel again and I get this blur of Luke who leans his head against me ... I always have this thing where I feel like I like someone or love someone and it's always at this moment when for a second of me knowing them it feels like they're looking for someone but they find someone else so soon and I'm standing somewhere with them watching them walk away or I realise that I'm not the right person even though I'm convinced that I am and I see that exact moment when they hold someone else's hand or like the time Luke Emma and me were all on Emma's bed and those two were lying length ways and I was sitting across the bed at the bottom and we were listening to music and I was thinking about something to do with the three of us and I think I said something about the music because it was around the time I think that music was still really important to me in the way that I wish it still was now and I remember not getting an answer to something I said while I was staring at some poster and I looked to the side and I hadn't got an answer because Emma and Luke had started kissing and it was their first kiss, I mean that I'd seen, and I could see that even though he'd tried to lift his leg up a tiny bit that

Luke had an erection and it had probably been there for a while and Emma was probably wet although I don't think I thought of that at the time but they both must have known something was going to happen and I'm trying really hard but I don't think that I can remember whether or not I knew that it was too and if I did maybe I just pretended against it or maybe one of the two had said something to me but I had tried to ignore it or maybe I had been so lost inside feeling jealous which is one of the reasons I think I might be a really bad person and I tried to forget everything that I had heard or whatever either of them had said to me because whenever people talk about love I think they must be getting it wrong because I don't feel loved in the way that I think that love is supposed to feel, so how can it be universal, or if it is, I mean, what does that mean for me ... then glitter smudged into skin losing its shine ... I wish the internet was made of plastic ... Luke's hand is dry dehydrated not drank in a while falling not quite asleep and things still speeding slowly ... Emma sitting on Alex's lap like in a porno rubbing between her legs // the laptop music sounds like knuckles cracking // Emma's spine stretching back and Alex's face scissored between her shoulder blades ... bbblinkinggg // Luke whispering to me and talking louder volume going up without him trying so it's my ears reminding me what room I'm in talking about his dad I can't tell what kind of things he feels he's lost which is stupid because I know he must miss his dad a lot, there's this certainty to what he feels. Picture of Luke curled up in a ball screaming, every time looks like close-ups like an MTV special about houses and rooms different sized rooms with corridors seen from the top so it looks like a flat version of that email and there's no joke at the end like inside a rat cage Alex is at the other side scrambling round the floor helping thoughts about that poster the pink is like sludge ... Alex's face is like a haunted house // yellow teeth dropping out, grime ... bits of flaked skin on the carpet peeling plants would die // The couple shouting one on the ground window spins thinking about people who know me but don't know me as a friend people I see around

131

people who recognize me I think about whether there's anyone who recognizes me regularly can't talk yellow smells /y/e/l/low//s/m/e/l/l/s all the music can ever be is distance same with Luke's face shit he's still talking I'm two seconds before I last looked thought he swapped to Alex // Alex's dick in my mouth aerial view in the dark winter's the kind of season to really get lost in // the laptop music like chandeliers // dirty pennies scattering ... taste of ash ... I've fallen to the side, liquids ... Luke is helping me passing me a glass of water ... trying to work out the closest I could be to him chests pushed together thinking about skin, friction // Alex's teeth falling out one by one going just out of view ... sirens so I pick myself up use a street name to balance knees are ripped or red at least like sores and puddles cold keep worrying that I need to use a telephone and that I don't recognize the people arguing // snows getting heavier real think about the corpse and its feathers frosting worms leaving actors fucking someone kicking the dead bird as hard as they can because they don't know who they are and it's nothing to do with being wrong I don't think because I guess death came first and this is all just static like a radio in a storm // snow spread out old computer game the earth could be on fire and my best friend at a funeral I don't know who I want to fuck or who I want to be and Emma has done nothing wrong in her life which makes her kinda perfect and I know that Alex and Luke are the same and they've not chose to think in this way I haven't chosen to think in this way I'm lucky and all the jealousy is fault and natural too which isn't impossible skeleton layers of tissue upon flesh before there's chance for any skin snow so constant it feels sharp hope there's no glass choking on all the ash can't tell if someone was just laughing seems like months since there was anything else there's hints of things being more skull maybe the snow is the music and I got things the wrong way round the bird wants to dig in the snow the bird wants to dig into the snow the bird flickering because I'm in the same place that I saw it took its blood to the funeral Craig's t-shirts have fonts on that I can't even read maybe the bands he likes barely exist and that's why they're so important I told Craig things that were true even though I didn't quite get past some girl saying things to him I think I've only even seen him four times in the flesh where does he hide in the day same kind of animals still sniffing round the bird frail spine lengthens Alex's mouth tongue at the base of Emma's ribs Luke's ribs rubbing against mine there are no ways to get as close as I feel I need to believe that people care this snow is so intense ... diagonal depending on where my eyes want to fall I'm being sick into a toilet have to put my hand in small circles of stained piss on the rim so there's something to hold onto pubic hair next to my finger I want to shit myself inside out // Emma shitting all over Alex's cock pushing herself upwards exploding into clouds or bubbles the ash I licked made me staring at the water spit on my chin Luke did say something to lighten the mood and I've pulled myself onto the sofa and I'm listening to him tapping his feet against the table and telling me why the music is so important because someone is taking everything apart and putting it together again in the same places but like bits of permanent snow that isn't wet of cold so I think like metal or something so thin you can't even tell what it's meant to be only it's important that everyone can tell that it was made on purpose and that someone made it rather than it being natural that email meant nothing so I think about things I've tried to // stare so hard till it looks like the snow is flying upwards and is coming from the ground // same corridor different rooms one room the next – constant – aerial view – birds eye view bird's eyes shut closed doors locked mucky cistern off white basin choking just bile chest pains Luke's chest cold his nipples hard fingers playing with them hand slipped up his t-shirt // face on damp blanket we're all walking in snow it's easy to stop worrying about people if you could forget how their faces are supposed to be, their faces ... feral savant sucking till cum rises ... I guess things heal but you'll still be staggering // snow makes the clouds disappear // every click and beat and swirl and click and pulse and blood of the music sounds hours away in this way that's closer than any of us every voice sounds so isolated desperate hungry clichéd impression cold terrified terrifying some skin split only small and I can't tell if it's mine names are changed around there's this spiral I realise how filthy my hands look hope the cut doesn't get infected can't remember anything more than now pathetic grave if you see it close up you build it using hundreds of little codes that end up turning into pictures and write about the sort of stuff you're interested in small things squeak in through cracks like worms soggy sores only thing that makes sense was when I turned it over and Luke was stoned think he's the same now smoking which is why I licked the ashtray and still about Alex's teeth could I swallow one of them me fucking Alex he's facing away we're both naked aerial view again if I was invisible through the corridor in another room looks like boxes held together by Sellotape gone brown curling my fingers scratching at his shoulders keeping his skin in place while his bones move forward so I'm thinking of a ripping sensation something's torn // greasy hands chipped tooth like hangnail ripped out of gummy fingertip exhausted palms searching all over Luke's body parting his cheeks shit smeared across Alex's groin dead birds falling feathers blown side to side dried blood last interviews Craig reading a message I think people like the attention I give them because they can tell I see something in them that other people don't even if I don't understand what it is or why I'm seeing it it makes people feel interesting and they send something back to me like signals they know what I like in them even if they doubt it's there but they can live with it and play up to it and believe what I believe in them that I can't see Emma feels less because Luke isn't letting her inside I want everything inside out sucking Luke's tongue with mine fucking his mouth with kisses chests so tight our ribs could snap gripping his dick through his jeans swallow like tinsel new bitter taste in my cheeks Emma's pussy squirting everywhere how do people start understanding like the people who seem pretty clear if people ask me a question Luke's dick is really big but he'd never talk about it know what to say straight away when they're talking about something important I try to stop listening because it drives me insane because I think people are lost and I keep telling myself that probably to make myself feel better I wonder if people ever have moments where the idea that they are the cause of everything that's going wrong around them and the people that they know that it's just fucking inescapable I'm thinking of something really bad but I can't quite remember the ... name? Things aren't being placed properly ... feral savant game show host like fluff or like stringy meat from something I might have ate stuck between or hanging from the back of my teeth really thin tiny rubbing my tongue across them feels like something to do with the music it's all the sounds the same like the sounds of something ripping paper Alex bucking away from me and having to take my dick out so I can cum on the base of his back his spine dinosaur jagged // so glad to be inside again // bite his teeth so hard until his or my teeth start to snap out and break // you realise how thin the line is I was doing something earlier in the day things have felt healthier? than this things can go out of sight so fast I remember someone telling me something about blind spots when there's something just out of the corner of your eye so the eyes just guess and cover it over with something it guess I might have that wrong ... "Can you hear that//?" "what?" "Can you hear that?//" "What?" "That ////?" "What???//" "Can you hear what?" "That." Head up air in through sweaty mouth tastes metallic real dry bottom row of my teeth hit the glass makes me think of first kisses nervous // Drink some of the water feels like really skinny twigs being pushed down my windpipe // I'm crying and I'm holding Luke's shoulders trying to pinpoint his eyes where to look work out makes me think of Emma when they've held me and I've been somewhere else those *of* are the private moments that people have when they don't think about being cruel I wasn't there I'm holding Luke's shoulders and I'm crying and I'm trying to work out what I'm saying my jaw feels numb we're a thousand places at once the music is like rushes "Are you – do you – do – you – are – you - ... ok?" so stupid again

135

can't even find it think maybe Luke is close to tears I think he's the other side of the room against the wall in a huddle the furthest away bird's eye view // A dead bird covered snow burial cremated under melting soggy ground paper cup turned transparent I want someone to tell me that they love me and I want to be able to believe that it's the same kind of love that I feel for other people that they never understand and can never bring themselves to give back to me, back to themselves // rodent through tunnels // email navigation sitting in this little room where the computer is left Luke can't say if he was asleep or just trying to hide from the stuff he was thinking about close the door and feels like temperature falls straight away black walls probably more green dark blue it's because of the light the computer is at the end of the bed have to sit right on the end it's not the right height so I sorta have to lean forward like I'm bigger than something lurch I wish I could keep all the things I hear and remember things like a hard drive maybe be able to see them as exactly what they are memory puts things in different shadows I think it's over an hour since I saw Alex he's still in that room unless another I think he just went to sleep when I went looking for Luke // there's this strange low light that I think is night doing what it can before it has to stop that's making a visual hum behind some shut blinds that its painted violet, there's a rim of sky blue round it // the screen glows in the dark like some kid that thinks it understands a grown up joke // it seems like there are way too many passwords to get right but I think it might just be one but it feels more important than before the picture I wanted to put on for myself has gone because of some copyright thing I know that because of the red writing that's underlined so now I'm a square with the outline silhouette filled grey of shoulders and torso just the top half of a person // the internet prefers me as a ghost // sudden burst of movement fingers part blind think about Emma's lips or Alex's ass or a bleeding cut in Luke's chest from friction started off as scabs picked ease fingers in dried bloody stings the clouds are more like video game than what they're meant to be: clouds dark purple navy blue fireworks that failed could stay floating around for years all their colours drained and dull and runny so they're just see through Alex's iPod is next to the keyboard push it to the side something about it makes me feel burnt hey so I guess it's probably really strange that I'm writing out of the blue like this especially since you don't images of some boy skateboarding really loud vicious music about destroying stuff hair I want to say is greasy but it isn't hangs down uncombed whatever the wheels are made of bashing to a stop on every ground should be should be me made of wood like trees people are not like trees can't cut them open don't see rings // too many guess because of impressions wondered about stuff about fathers and my friends dad just died do you think ever think that the internet is haunted I do and there was just this music that maybe was made by the internet as well but that all just seems too much to take in so i shut the door and now it's only silence just a few little clicks on the keyboard assembling w/o/r/d/s putting l/e/t/t/e/r/s words and/l/e/t/r/s together// ghosts on the internet must look a lot different to ghosts in real life unless it's a video on Youtube or something but then they'd be different if you put your eyes right up against the screen watery and strained ghosts are robotic I get lost these corridors are different to the place where we are it's hard trying to work out what a aerial view of the internet would look like maybe a hologram I saw this video of a hologram I think it was some art thing some skull floating in a museum or gallery or website or funeral I saw a video of this I start typing things // looking for skulls and bones in cyberspace, like a buried body, I guess if you're cremated on the internet then that must mean you turn into bitmap // bitmap crematorium // I felt bad like all the people at the funeral were looking for a reaction so I didn't look at anyone maybe I wanted the same from Luke maybe that's why he wasn't looking at Emma she didn't want a reaction she was just doing the right thing which makes me feel bad because I can see that I was the most selfish person there even if it's just because I was sad so that makes me think maybe I'm not a bad person but that I just sometimes want things that aren't one hundred percent good which means there is no such thing as a good or a bad person still feels like this is all too late though something has been lost that we never had in the first place something has gone when I think of acid I think about something that can burn holes in stuff, I think of coronas // Picture myself talking to Emma – yeah – are you guys having fun? – stuff feels so fucked up – how are things fucked up? – it's hard to – just try, if things are fucked up – then I feel like an advert so I have to stop neck cracks rush look to the side and think about being inside whatever I can hear // try again tip eyes around looking at Craig's photographs I only know him paper thin like this fixed pose pixels about youth I feel scared of how perfect he looks and I know he hasn't got a clue so I've seen you a couple of times and I want to say that I found you by accident but bullshit because I tried really hard to find you I want to think that you might need me because you're lonely and I'm talking like a mirror with a big crack down the middle of it, or like the CD case, I like how you don't seem corrupt like fashion or what people do in each other's arms this is just a rough attempt, approximate, I imagine all these things so I guess you're just a hologram and I've found the ghost and pile of bones I knew would be there on the internet maybe the hologram is from me and I'm just projecting it against you so I can see it which makes you something a bit like a black wall and I thought that email was really special when I say you're a black wall that's not meant in a cruel way if the wall wasn't there I wouldn't be able to see any of this stuff I think people use each other to see things that they hope are going to be beautiful and they can't see them if they're on their own and because I really feel hopeless and like there's no real point me having this love if I feel so pathetic maybe I'm just getting reflections of myself like when you walk past a shop and wonder why someone is looking back and then there's that one second of fear when you see it's you I just want to know if everyone feels like that or if it's just me and you're so beautiful when I think about fucking you it's not just because of

138

your body and it's not just because of mine I want to meet someone I can make promises for that will mean more than just friends that care about each other this isn't making sense, the promises ... I want to apologize every second of every day for the rest of my life, I'll need to ... people can use computers to make photographs look more real than the things they were taken to remind people about ... in this light you look holy ... you're probably asleep have no idea how much you mean because you're dreaming which makes you far off but I'm here this must be what it's like watching trees fall with no one to hear them... couple more girls are in love with you looks like one you might know the other just some illusion another country a hint or something more logos on her page yours is pretty simple there are a million different codes to learn if you want to show someone what you're really like how you see yourself how you get closer to what you want people to look at and notice all the important things that you can't convince yourself of try and make the pictures move make it more like flesh more like something I could watch rather than just think about when I've watched you I've barely been thinking when I've watched you I've felt so removed from myself like you're all these people that I didn't get the chance to meet in terms of life you're not really that much younger than me people can be a hundred but there's this huge gap between what I think you might be and how much I want you to be and you to be it whatever that is I've been thinking about to me and it's not about being selfish because if only you were exactly what I'm thinking about then I know all I would want to do is give you everything start feeling sad as soon as I realise that guess because I don't have anything to offer you look at you listen to you find ways to make you feel better try and understand you more than the people who would just wanna fuck you or use you to make themselves feel more complicated by putting you as this thing that needs them I need you I need someone I need anyone I know I was a kid because I think I still feel the same just different because of things I've seen or let go of but I can tell you're closer to that the first time someone screams

139

is the worst because there's nothing to compare that to I know that if I saw an old man in a hospital screaming then I'd bet it was like the millionth time he'd screamed in his life makes me think about Luke's dad's heart exploding or whatever and how the pain was different but how he probably could deal with what was going on even if his body was going against him I don't know what Luke has done with the ashes the way he was with his dad was always // aerial view still a room and everything could just be summed up with squares and rectangles this whole place reading through every little thing about you and some of it is not making sense someone saying that they miss you someone saying they wish you were there for them to talk to someone saying they can't believe what has happened someone saying they would do anything to bring you back someone saying they're hurting a lot someone saying they don't see the point in living someone saying that you need to be happy in your new place someone saying that they miss you but they'll see you again some day someone swearing someone saying fuck and about how much they hate something feels like something has gone badly wrong something feels intensely frightening reading more trying to // try again // eyes flip //swallow // twigs in throat// rearrange take in try to rearrange again and take in look at the time not can imagine how night can end so easily still dark but something on the move rearrange ... log in and then log out again can't tell what you've read so dunno have you had chance to see what I said to you this is so horrific I can barely stand it think about earlier hours since I vomited in the bathroom everything is saying that Craig's friends are going to miss him now that he's gone everything's saying that it's been sudden the internet is trying to tell me about ghosts weird how I knew that anyway just expecting different bodies maybe you never know what you're looking for until you find it and have chance to realise a little bit more about who you are and why this is happening there are split seconds when every single little tiny thing in every moment that ever passes joins up and I can see but I'm so desperate trying to make sense of it that it's like sand running through my dirty tired lost fingers I'm so fucking paranoid that I dismantle love before it even starts // ashes are whatever you want them to be probably because the wind can blow them anywhere and they're a hundred people mixed up at once – that seems hopeless // I think I hear people shouting no just one person no none just none // If Emma was here naked I wouldn't do half of the things that I'm thinking about – I don't think I'd know what to do – all I would want is for her to feel good – forget about me // I can't tell the difference between dust and glitter, I just want to put my fingers on the keyboard and let them holddddddddddddddddddddddddd downnnnnnnnnnnnn and just watch the letters build up on the screen then press enter and see where I'm searching // I don't understand the idea of privacy everything should be private or nothing at all somewhere in the middle just doesn't work a song starts playing and I jump guess I've not been looking at Craig's page for very long because the song has just started people put songs on their page to try and give clues to what kind of people they are Craig's song is some punk thing I think that he's probably noticed Luke in the street at some point which must be true because I've noticed Craig I don't think Craig has noticed me I click on something that makes the music stop because right now I think music has done everything that it could in this situation and that makes me feel like a liar // When I was sick it feels like someone was watching can't have been Luke I think I was in a ball so it must have been Alex why can't I stop seeing him naked whenever I think about him if he was watching then I might have got vomit on him when I was asking for help if I realised that he was there // I'm so itchy and numb my body feels like fruit that's been bruised // So many people are saying goodbye to Craig I can't quite grasp what's happened or I'm choosing to look in the wrong place because otherwise things are just too scary – that's something to do with some book that I saw e/a/r/l/i/e/r/ in the other room the other square aerial view feathers snow worms dried blood never thought about looking them in the eye before I just

want to hold hands and not worry about the other person noticing
... the clock says something that I don't even want to go into // in
all this time nobody has missed us // They don't understand what
I see in you and I'm not sure if I should really care // I don't think
I would really ever want to sleep with Luke or Emma or Alex I
know that I wouldn't which is weird because all the things I think
are still not lies because they feel different // I think I could probably
sleep with Alex because he definitely feels different to the others –
that's not a good thing ... I // I think about the word acid it barely
means anything apart from broken bits of glass if you keep crushing
maybe that's where the glitter comes from it's just stuff through lots
of different angles until the angles are too small to work out what
you're seeing or which reflection is the m/o/s/t/ ... w/h/a/t/e/v/e/r
... I think I missed Craig and left things too late because he's not
going to read what I wrote now unless they have the internet in ...
some thoughts you just have to stop ... all the people who are sad
about death seem to be from America – all the teenage girls who
miss Craig because of what his face looked like – it's crazy because
you can't just press Undo // there are no people from round here
talking to Craig I reload the page to try and look at things again
because I've just been staring and after a while it's just like if you
keep repeating a word to yourself it starts to sound different and
mean nothing yourself yourself yourself yourself yourself yourself
yourself yourself yourself yourself yourself yourself yourself
yourself yourself yourself yourself yourself yourself yourself
yourself yourself yourself yourself yourself yourself yourself
yourself yourself yourself yourself yourself yourself and you start
to doubt that you're saying the word right or if the letters really add
up to that or have you had things wrong from the start so I press
Refresh Craig is here again the photo appears first and then the
punk song starts which now means punk music is a funeral march
sounds like a skull shaking bones must be fragile wonder how much
effort it would take a computer couldn't smash a skull // one new
comment from someone who isn't American saying something

about fakeness Craig can't answer this girl says Craig is a liar I don't know her ideas about death can't quite read what she says she's taken her photo from above so it makes her hair look huge she's wearing this black and white dress like a chess board her eyes have a ton of makeup round them like when you make writing bold to make a point or so it's easier for people to work out where to look she writes something about a friend who isn't Craig calls Craig a name calls him a liar says that he's a fake says his pictures aren't real or they aren't his or they aren't true I don't think I stopped the punk music properly her idea of dying is gone makes me think about mine she says Craig is pathetic that he must be really ugly says that he's using her friend's pictures says another name not Craig guess she means her friend who isn't Craig and who Craig isn't maybe the boy I see in the street doesn't even exist on the internet must do because his pictures have come from somewhere I don't know shit my picture is just a cartoon so I'm no one too who have I told everything to if Craig isn't dead and wasn't even alive that can't really matter people get confused trying to work out what people are seeing in them so they forget what they see in themselves maybe people are all just like glass or something on the inside so all the organs and stuff are like plastic toys in a science museum for kids loneliness and sadness and grieving and just wanting to be held by someone can't be bad because I think it must be everywhere because otherwise people wouldn't all be feeling like this don't ask me how I know they are because I'm just in one room which I've been thinking about as if it were a box and I'm just reading what all the other people have been saying from their spaces so I can't tell for sure but I just get this feeling that at least one thing must be true // I can't choose which of my memories to believe // I can see the sun coming up

143

14

Hello?
Hey.
Hi. Are you ok?
...
It's late.
It's early.
Yeah ... umm ... yeah.
It's both.
Yeah.
...
What are you doing?
Nothing.
Where are you?
Here.
Still up?
Yeah.
Are you sure you're ok?
No.
...
...
What's wrong?
I don't know.
I'm worried about you.
Why?
I don't know.
It's cool to talk to you.
Are we talking?
Yeah. Kinda. Yeah. We're talking.
What's it like where you are?

It's ... it's just here.

What's it like?

Late. I'm tired.

So it's tiring there?

What? No. I'm tired. Here isn't ... maybe it is.

Being here, where I am, wears me out.

You should sleep. I don't even know what the time is.

It feels different here.

How?

I don't know. You're not here. That makes a difference.

I'm talking to you. So I'm kinda there.

Yeah.

I wish you were.

Why?

It would help. I could ask you things.

Ask me now.

Not like that. I haven't got any questions that I want to ask. But if you were here then I'd be able to find things out. Otherwise it's just like looking at a picture. It doesn't feel real.

...

It feels like what it would feel like talking to a ghost.

I'm not a ghost.

You're not here.

It makes a difference. I said that.

If I was there what would you want me to do?

I don't know.

Would you want to fuck me?

I don't know. Yeah.

Do you think that I'd like you to fuck me?

Yeah. You would like it.

You sound sad.

Can words be sad? I mean, to themselves?

Every word is sad.

No. I don't think I'm sad. I don't think I'd know what to do with you. Things are always different when people are naked. Maybe I am sad.

Would you be scared of me?

No. It's just different. Things that I think are not the same as things that I do.

What do you think about?

Some of the things that I do. Some of the things that I don't do. Some of the things that I think about but do that are different. Other stuff.

What other stuff?

How much do you think about death?

I don't know. I've not really thought too much – why? How much do you think about death?

Too much. Not enough. Hardly ever. All the time.

I want to be there.

...

Do you want me there?

I think you need everyone to want you.

What?

I think you need everyone to want you. You want people to need you.

Do you need me?

I don't know how to answer that. I don't know if I need you.

Do you want me to be where you are?

What do you want me to say?

You think that I'm going to say that I don't want you to need me.

I don't know what you're going to say.

Do you know what you think I'm going to say?

So you get it?

Yeah – two different things.

This is so confusing.

Yeah. Everything is confusing.

I'd be more confused if people were straight forward though.

Yeah – you mean if things are easier?

Things aren't easy.

I know – I was just saying …

Yeah, sorry.

Are you angry about things?

What things?

Anything I guess.

Probably. Can't say for sure though.

…

Are you?

Angry?

Yeah.

Same as you. I don't know. Sometimes I think I am.

Are there things you wish you could take back?

Probably. But it's impossible to say those kinds of things really. It's easy to say them. But it's impossible to know if it's true. You know?

Yeah. I think we're the same.

Haha.

When it comes to those things.

Yeah I know what you meant. Sorry.

It's late.

Should I leave you to try and … sleep?

I don't know.

Do you think you'll be able to sleep?

Now?

Yeah.

I don't know.

Do you think you know me?

No.

What do you think you'd have to know about me to know me properly?

You mean … what do you mean?

I don't know. What don't you know about me?

You mean like specific details?

I guess. Maybe.

I don't know. That's kinda impossible.

Impossible to work out?

I think that's what I mean.

I guess you just get an idea of someone, based on …

…

I don't know. Based on your own way of … seeing things? Does that makes sense?

Maybe.

You see people how you want to see them maybe.

You get clues.

Yeah. Enough rope to hang yourself!

What? What do you mean?

It's just a saying – haven't you heard people say that before?

Who says it?

I dunno. People just do.

It's crazy – like suicide, right?

Yeah I guess … but it isn't actually about that.

It's weird that it doesn't really mean what the words themselves actually mean.

Yeah. I think that's like everything though. Literally illiterate.

Yeah. Do you think that's why everyone is so fucked up?

Maybe. It probably has a lot to do with it.

But I guess there are a million reasons for that.

Yeah, probably.

Do you feel fucked up?

Do you think I'm fucked up?

I don't know – you're not here. So at this moment, I'm tired and I only have pictures in my head to go on. It seems like that's probably not the right way to do it.

Have a guess – I don't mind. I won't feel like you're … I dunno … being unfair about me or anything …

I think I kinda presume that you must be fucked up a little bit.

And I know it sounds weird but I think that that's probably half of the reason why I feel so attracted to you.

I sometimes think that's the only reason why people are attracted to me.

Really?

Yeah.

Why?

I can just tell. People assume I'm fucked up. And it makes them want to have me.

Have people told you that?

You have.

I mean other people.

Not really. Not how you have. Some have said almost the same things. Most of the time I can just tell by the way people act. The things they say to me. How they act around me.

How do you know it isn't just you?

You mean am I paranoid?

No – aren't people just attracted to you because you're attractive? I mean physically.

Do you think I am?

Do you?

I can't tell. I've tried, I guess to some people, yeah, but that's not what I mean. Have you thought about fucking me?

You must know I have.

How would I know?

Just from who you are and who I am – I've thought about it a lot, yeah.

Are you thinking about me now?

Yeah … I've got this picture of you …

Yeah. But whatever.

I can't make up my mind what I'm thinking when I think about you.

You're boring sometimes. That's not meant as an insult. I think I'm boring too.

I know.

15

I wake up. I've not slept. It took a few hours of just sitting. Breathing's like patchwork.

I try to look around. My eyes are glazed so I give up. It's like trying to look through a couple of those Ice Glacier sweets that kids suck to get over car sickness. A screensaver floats around the monitor at the end of the bed. I stretch and I feel covered with lots of small gentle aches. I have this image of a piece of cold meat being folded in half like someone closing a book.

The first thing I notice is how quiet it is. I feel cold. I grab a fist of duvet and try to pull as much over myself as I can. It takes *a* three attempts and I have to rearrange my foot before I'm covered properly. I'm facing the wall. It's painted this sky blue colour, and when my eyes start to relax I can see tiny little patterns and waves still bouncing around. My vision is still a little bit like liquid, but it's more subtle now, rippling.

I close my eyes and get this rush that's like static and I realise I'm not going to sleep. My jaw's tired from grinding against itself. My gums are probably sore.

I stretch again, this time I add a yawn which brings a shiver. I'm cold. I hate the fact that I have a really short attention span because otherwise I know I'd be able to lie here and ... heal? I feel like someone's hollowed me out.

Drugs can make some things really clear; like the confusion of stuff itself. It's like there's a switch or when people talk about a fine line, I think I know exactly what they mean. My jeans or the mattress feels damp. I put my hand between my legs to check if I've wet myself. It sounds dumb but I wouldn't be surprised. It must just be sweat. I think I'd feel better if I felt clean. I never feel clean if I've slept at someone else's place.

I know that the room next to me is the bathroom but that would mean leaving this one, which I don't know if I want to do or not. In some ways I know I have to, but I don't know what's been happening for the last nine hours, I don't know what I've been saying and opening the door would be like – yeah, just that.

I have all these fears. They seem to work better where they are, but that's scary too.

Trying to piece things together is hard. My throat is really sore which means that I was probably sick. I had a feeling I was but I had lots of other feelings that I can't be sure of so I can't take anything for granted. The main thing I remember feeling is this huge sense of guilt. I know that I was to blame for a lot of things that I might not get to think about properly again. Fuck it. I don't know. I shiver some more.

My dick's hard. It's strange that even when I feel so weird, there's still this horniness. I think my body and brain both have different motives to each other. I move onto my back. I stretch out my legs and undo the button and zip on my jeans. I wiggle myself a little so that I move the jeans down to around my knees. I pull my cock and my balls out of my underwear so that the waistline rests just underneath my testicles. At first I just hold my dick, feel how warm it is. It feels really glossy, or greasy like the cover of a movie magazine, and my hand has pins and needles from where I've been lying on it, so it feels pretty much like someone else's which seems to suit me right now.

I sit up quickly which makes me dizzy – which I note for future reference. I waggle the mouse and then lay back down. The screensaver has gone and there's a picture of Craig on the screen. I have this weird shadow in my mind of me looking at his profile a few hours ago – a sense of it anyway, because the memories and what was going on or how I perceived it is still very much like a cloud or condensation still. Whatever. I don't want to think about anything like that. It's too – close, I think.

I stare at Craig's face and start to wank myself off. In the picture he's wearing a black t-shirt that's a size too big for him. He looks amazing. When I first saw porn I was disappointed. I've always been more turned on by clues. I just never worked out what I have to solve. It's a puzzle without a picture.

I look at the place where Craig is. I'm so not there. Even in the way I'm looking at it – I'm totally somewhere else.

Photographs are strange. People think they can make them closer to stuff that happened a long time ago, but they can't. Even if I was in that photograph with Craig, then I would still be millions of miles away from him. Photographs don't keep people in touch with the past. They just do a much better job than what people think memory is supposed to do. They're more reliable than thoughts. Even in the pictures I have on my wall, I don't think they make me closer to my friends or anything. I just like having them so that I can look at my friends.

There's no way that I could ever be close to Craig. I'm barely close to myself. I always feel like I'm keeping myself at a distance somehow. Maybe I don't trust myself. I feel like I'm probably an ok person sometimes. I don't know what that means.

I keep closing my eyes and then looking back at the picture for reference. I lean back and occasionally waggle the mouse with my toes so that the screensaver doesn't appear again. Craig's t-shirt has got a logo on that I can't make out. It's for some band, I'm pretty certain of that. I try to imagine what music's like for him. I'm only a little older but it feels like trying to imagine a totally different world – that's got nothing to do with age, that's more to do with the things I feel that I've misplaced. It can happen to anyone, and earlier.

Sometimes I feel like there's been a big fire and it's destroyed all the reasons about why things were important to me, but somehow I missed it happening. I lost things in that fire.

I give up masturbating and zip myself back up. It feels like I'm running out of ideas. This is too much.

I feel scared to click on the part of the screen where it says Messages, in case I see that Craig has read and now replied to what

I sent him. Ideally I wanted it deleted before he opened it. It feels like so long ago. It feels like years since I was talking to Luke, or getting paranoid about Alex, or calibrating Emma.

I decide that I have to leave the room and I stand up. I close the website down in case anyone walks in and sees a picture of Craig or sees that I have a profile on the website, because that would just feel confusing. I open the door and get colder straight away. The creaking sounds louder than it is. The silence makes it sound like shrieking. I slip through as soon as the gap between the door and the doorframe is big enough. The first thing I do is walk into the bathroom. I'm almost surprised that I don't see a ghost of myself curled up next to the toilet, crying and vomiting. I lock the door and then put my hands on the sink and stare into the bathroom mirror. The first thing I notice is that the glass is all smudged, like it hasn't been cleaned in a while. I look pretty much the same as I always do except my skin looks shinier than normal so I splash some water on it and wipe a facecloth hard against my skin, especially the bits either side of my nose because they feel the greasiest.

I look at the colour of the piss as it leaves me and falls, trickles, squirts and then starts coming properly, into the toilet. Orange. The idea of something coming from inside me is strange. Last night I felt more connected to my body in the sense that I wasn't part of it, but I was it. This morning I feel like a hologram.

There's a sound. It pricks me. I walk down the tiny corridor that connects all the rooms and makes it feel like one of those mazes that people put in cages to entertain hamsters. I push down the door handle to Alex's spare room really slowly, in case the noise wasn't as prominent as I thought it was. Alex is asleep. He's lying on the floor face down, all sprawled out. There are couple of t-shirts and a backpack piled on top of each other; he's resting his head on them. The room feels like it was messier last night, or that it should feel messier now. It just feels still.

I walk back down the hamster tunnel and open the other door in the same way that I've opened every other door so far. There's a gentle, full, breathing sound, and a slight snore coming from the sofa. I walk to the back of it and look down at Luke. It's so easy to believe that he used to be a child; I mean it's so easy to believe at this exact moment in time. Right now he's curled up. He's lying on his right hand side, facing into the settee. His eyes are shut. His mouth is open just wide enough for me to see his front teeth. His lips wobble every so often, like just this second. I think that the one thing that doesn't change about people is the way that they sleep. Maybe their dreams change, but I'm pretty sure that Luke looked exactly like this when he used to sleep as a kid. There's something about that that's really amazing, when I think about it, so I try not to, because ... I don't know ... I just don't want to hurt anymore.

Luke's clothes look like they've been on his body for more than just one night. His body hasn't had chance to breathe without them overnight – that'll be why. The back of his t-shirt – which is black – has rode up just enough so that a tiny part of his back is peeking out – this skin looks so effortless that it slays me.

So I'm just standing still. I'm not sure if I could be doing anything else. It feels like all this time I'm trying so hard not to think about a million things and with the effort I'm actually putting into that, I could actually be doing all of those things. All of those things that for some reason my brain doesn't want to let near me right now.

I play on the computer for a few hours. Occasionally I stand in the room where Luke's sleeping. I don't think too much about Alex, because I'm fairly confident that he's fine sound asleep.

Alex wakes up before Luke and walks into the room where I'm perched on the bed, messing around on the computer. He's wearing the same red t-shirt as last night, and just his boxer shorts. His eyes look half closed. He scratches his head, does a half grimace, half grin and says "Fuck."

I walk with Alex into the room where Luke's sleeping. Alex stands on one foot and leans over the back of the sofa where Luke's sleeping, a lot less carefully than I've been doing up to this point, and laughs.

I watch Alex's hand shakily tip a heaped teaspoon of sugar into a mug of tea that he's just made. The kettle sounded brutal. He puts about seven or eight spoonfuls into the cup, and tosses the teaspoon into the sink.

He says: "Hey feel free to stick around for as long as you like, or if you want to get going that's cool too. Do whatever you want. I need a few more hours sleep." Alex goes back to bed.

I think it's around 3 in the afternoon already.

I play on the internet some more. The only thing that I eat or drink is a cup of hot chocolate which hurts my teeth.

I think about going home and feel like crying.

I think I must have been dozing. I hear a door slam. I go and check the front room. Luke's gone.

16

I took a walk round suburbia tonight. A lot of stuff felt like it was being shot through coloured filters, mostly black and orange. Everything was set out so neatly; that and the silence made it feel like a diorama. The leaves of the uniformed bushes and trees that line certain streets and stand like guards at the top of people's drives looked more beautiful than they do when the sun shines on them. The greens are a lot richer, like at night colour is saved for connoisseurs and insomniacs. The primary colours of middle of the range cars seem tested by the mix of hazy light and blackness. It's like you can squeeze something really beautiful and unexpected out of the darkness. If this is a diorama then it feels like one that hasn't been completed and has just been left as it is. Whoever stuck the glue in place and planted the symmetrical streets has moved onto something else or just gotten bored. You can tell there's something missing.

THE END